MARK TWAIN

TOM SAWYER ABROAD

::

TOM SAWYER, DETECTIVE

THE MARK TWAIN LIBRARY

The Library offers for the first time popular editions of Mark Twain's best works just as he wanted them to be read. These moderately priced volumes, faithfully reproduced from the California scholarly editions and printed on acid-free paper, are sparingly annotated and include all the original illustrations that Mark Twain commissioned and enjoyed.

"Huck waited for no particulars. He sprang away
and sped down the hill as fast as his
legs could carry him."

—THE ADVENTURES OF TOM SAWYER

"WE CATCHED A LOT OF THE NICEST FISH YOU EVER SEE"

MARK TWAIN

TOM SAWYER ABROAD

∷

TOM SAWYER, DETECTIVE

Foreword and Notes by
John C. Gerber

Text established by
Terry Firkins

University of California Press

Berkeley   Los Angeles   London

These Mark Twain Library texts of "Tom Sawyer Abroad" and "Tom Sawyer, Detective" are, for the most part, photographic reproductions of the texts published in *The Adventures of Tom Sawyer; Tom Sawyer Abroad; and Tom Sawyer, Detective*, ed. John C. Gerber, Paul Baender, and Terry Firkins (University of California Press, 1980), which was approved by the Center for Editions of American Authors (CEAA). Portions of each text have been reset to correct errors and to accommodate the original illustrations by Daniel Carter Beard and A. B. Frost. The reset portions have been proofread in accord with the standards of the CEAA. Mark Twain's typescript of chapters 1–10 of "Tom Sawyer, Detective" is MS P370A, which was donated to the Department of Special Collections, Kenneth Spencer Research Library, University of Kansas, by the late Milton F. Barlow of Prairie Village, Kansas. On behalf of the Library, permission to make use of this document in editing the text has been graciously extended to the Mark Twain Project by Alexandra Mason, Spencer Librarian. Editorial work on all texts was made possible by generous grants from the United States Office of Education and from the Research Materials Program of the National Endowment for the Humanities.

University of California Press
Berkeley and Los Angeles
University of California Press, Ltd.
London

Twain, Mark, 1835–1910.
  Tom Sawyer Abroad; and, Tom Sawyer, Detective.
  (The Mark Twain Library)
  I. Gerber, John C. ˝II. Twain, Mark, 1835–1910. Tom Sawyer, Detective. 1982. III. Title. IV. Series: Twain, Mark, 1835–1910. Mark Twain Library.
PS1320.A2G47 1982 818'.409
81-40325
ISBN 0-520-04560-2
ISBN 0-520-04561-0 (pbk.)

Manufactured in the United States of America.

1 2 3 4 5 6 7 8 9 0

The Mark Twain Library is designed by Steve Renick.

CONTENTS

ILLUSTRATIONS

FOREWORD

Published in 1894, *Tom Sawyer Abroad* is one of Mark Twain's major ventures into science fiction. In it he resurrects the three characters so popular in *Adventures of Huckleberry Finn*—Tom Sawyer, Huckleberry Finn, and Jim—and sends them on a balloon trip to Africa. The balloon is less ingeniously engineered than the space ships in present-day films and science fiction, but its wings and fans can propel it a hundred miles an hour in still air and three hundred miles an hour with a stiff tail wind.

Although he had previously toyed with the idea of a balloon adventure, Mark Twain clearly got the idea for this particular story from Jules Verne's *Five Weeks in a Balloon* (1869). From it he adapted such episodes as stopping at an oasis, encountering a lion, using the ladder for rescues, seeing a mirage, and hovering above a caravan while a sandstorm sweeps over it and entombs both people and camels. Yet the antics of Tom and Huck and Jim make the book unmistakably Mark Twain's. Tom is again the manager, the one with information and imagination. Huck is still the one with a literal mind and common sense, and Jim, though the oldest, is once more the most limited in experience and the most burdened by superstition. Tom despairs of ever having an intelligent conversation with his two companions, and they in turn often feel that their arguments have gotten the better of Tom. Popular in its time, *Tom Sawyer Abroad* is still enjoyed for its humor and its fantasy, for the disagreements of the "erronorts," and, of course, for Huck's marvelously colorful language.

Tom Sawyer, Detective (1896) is Mark Twain's best-known detective story. It is based on Steen Steenson Blicher's novel *The Minister of Veilby* (1829), a fictionalized account of a famous seventeenth-century Danish murder. By transferring the locale to the Phelps farm described in *Huckleberry Finn*, Mark Twain is able once more to use Huck as narrator and Tom Sawyer as the central character. He is also able to insert such favorite devices as male twins, a false deaf-mute, the fear of ghosts, swindles perpetrated on the innocent, mistaken identity, and a dramatic backwoods trial.

In *Tom Sawyer* and *Huckleberry Finn* Tom had occasionally acted "detective fashion," but in this book he performs throughout as a youthful imitation of the immensely popular Sherlock Holmes, with Huck as a counterpart of Dr. Watson. To everyone's wonderment Tom deduces who the murderer is and where the jewels are hidden. Characteristically, Mark Twain cannot resist exaggerating the events and building up the climax until they become ridiculous. As a result, *Tom Sawyer, Detective* is not only a detective story but also a burlesque of detective stories. Huck catches the spirit of the whole narrative when he says, after Tom produces the stolen diamonds, "Well, sir, if there'd been a brass band to bust out some music, then, it would 'a' been just the perfectest thing I ever see, and Tom Sawyer he said the same."

John C. Gerber

MARK TWAIN

TOM SAWYER
ABROAD

For as much as thirty years he'd been the only man in the village that had a ruputation—I mean, a ruputation for being a traveler, and of course he was mortal proud of it, and it was reckoned that in the course of that thirty years he had told about that journey over a million times and enjoyed it every time, and now comes along a boy not quite fifteen and sets everybody gawking and admiring over *his* travels, and it just give the poor old thing the jim-jams. It made him sick to listen to Tom and hear the people say "My land!" "Did you ever!" "My goodness sakes alive!" and all them sorts of things, but he couldn't pull away from it, any more than a fly that's got its hind leg fast in the molasses. And always when Tom come to a rest, the poor old cretur would chip in on *his* same old travels and work them for all they was worth, but they was pretty faded and didn't go for much, and it was pitiful to see. And then Tom would take another innings, and then the old man again—and so on, and so on, for an hour and more, each trying to sweat out the other.

You see, Parsons's travels happened like this. When he first got to be postmaster and was green in the business, there was a letter come for somebody he didn't know, and there wasn't any such person in the village. Well, he didn't know what to do nor how to act, and there the letter stayed and stayed, week in and week out, till the bare sight of it give him the dry gripes. The postage wasn't paid on it, and that was another thing to worry about. There wasn't any way to collect that ten cents, and he reckoned the Gov'ment would hold him responsible for it and maybe turn him out besides, when they found he hadn't collected it. Well at last he couldn't stand it any longer. He couldn't sleep nights, he couldn't eat, he was thinned down to a shadder, yet he dasn't ask anybody's advice, for the very person he asked for the advice might go back on him and let the Gov'ment know about that letter. He had the letter buried under the floor, but that didn't do no good; if he happened to see a person standing over the place it give him the cold shivers and loaded him up with suspicions, and he would set up that night till the town was still and dark and then he would sneak there and get it out and bury it in another place. Of course people got to avoiding him, and shaking their heads and whispering, because, the way he was looking and acting, they judged he had killed somebody or done something they didn't know what, and if he had been a stranger they would a lynched him.

Well, as I was saying, it got so he couldn't stand it any longer; so he made up his mind to pull out for Washington and just go to the President of the United States and make a clean breast of the whole thing, not keeping back an atom, and then fetch the letter out and lay her down before the whole Gov'ment and say, "Now, there she is, do with me what you're a mind to, though as heaven is my judge I am an innocent man and not deserving of the full penalties of the law, and leaving behind me a family which must starve and yet ain't had a thing to do with it, which is the truth and I can swear to it."

So he done it. He had a little wee bit of steamboating, and some stage-coaching, but all the rest of the way was horseback, and took him three weeks to get to Washington. He saw lots of land, and lots of villages, and four cities. He was gone most eight weeks, and there never was such a pow-wow in the village as when he got back. His travels made him the greatest man in all that region, and the most talked about; and people come from as much as thirty miles back in the country, and from over in the Illinois bottoms, too, just to look at him—and there they'd stand and gawk, and he'd gabble. You never see anything like it.

Well, there wasn't any way, now, to settle which was the greatest traveler; some said it was Nat, some said it was Tom. Everybody allowed that Nat had seen the most longitude, but they had to give in that whatever Tom was short in longitude he had made up in latitude and climate. It was about a stand-off; so both of them had to whoop-up their dangersome adventures, and try to get ahead that way. That bullet-wound in Tom's leg was a tough thing for Nat Parsons to buck against, but he done the best he could; done it at a disadvantage, too, for Tom didn't set still, as he'd orter done, to be fair, but always got up and santered around and worked his limp whilst Nat was painting up the adventure that he had one day in Washington; for Tom he never let go that limp after his leg got well, but practiced it nights at home, and kept it as good as new, right along.

Nat's adventure was like this; and I will say this for him, that he *did* know how to tell it. He could make anybody's flesh crawl and turn pale and hold his breath when he told it, and sometimes women and girls got so faint they couldn't stick it out. Well, it was this way, as near as I remember:

He come a-loping into Washington and put up his horse and

shoved out to the President's house with his letter, and they told him the President was up to the Capitol and just going to start for Philadelphia—not a minute to lose if he wanted to catch him. Nat most dropped, it made him so sick. His horse was put up, and he didn't know what to do. But just then along comes a nigger driving an old ramshackly hack, and he see his chance. He rushes out and shouts—

"A half a dollar if you git me to the capitol in a half an hour, and a quarter extra if you do it in twenty minutes!"

"Done!" says the nigger.

Nat he jumped in and slammed the door and away they went, a-ripping and a-tearing and a-bumping and a-bouncing over the roughest road a body ever see, and the racket of it was something awful. Nat passed his arms through the loops and hung on for life and death, but pretty soon the hack hit a rock and flew up in the air and the bottom fell out, and when it come down Nat's feet was on the ground, and he see he was in the most desperate danger if he couldn't keep up with the hack. He was horrible scared, but he laid into his work for all he was worth, and hung tight to the arm-loops and made his legs fairly fly. He yelled and shouted to the driver to stop, and so did the crowds along the street, for they could see his legs a-spinning along under the coach and his head and shoulders bobbing inside, through the windows, and knowed he was in awful danger; but the more they all shouted the more the nigger whooped and yelled and lashed the horses and said, "Don't you fret, I's gwyne to git you dah in time, boss, I's gwyne to do it sho'!" for you see *he* thought they was all hurrying him up, and of course he couldn't hear anything for the racket he was making. And so they went ripping along, and everybody just petrified and cold to see it; and when they got to the Capitol at last it was the quickest trip that ever was made, and everybody said so. The horses laid down, and Nat dropped, all tuckered out; and then they hauled him out and he was all dust and rags and barefooted; but he was in time, and just in time, and caught the President and give him the letter and everything was all right and the President give him a free pardon on the spot, and Nat give the nigger two extra quarters instead of one, because he could see that if he hadn't had the hack he wouldn't a got there in time, nor anywhere near it.

It *was* a powerful good adventure, and Tom Sawyer had to work his bullet-wound mighty lively to hold his own and keep his end up against it.

Well, by and by Tom's glory got to paling down gradualy, on accounts of other things turning up for the people to talk about, first a horse-race, and on top of that a house afire, and on top of that the circus, and on top of that a big auction of niggers, and on top of that the eclipse, and that started a revival, same as it always does, and by that time there warn't no more talk about Tom to speak of, and you never see a person so sick and disgusted. Pretty soon he got to worrying and fretting right along, day in and day out, and when I asked him what *was* he in such a state about, he said it most broke his heart to think how time was slipping away, and him getting older and older, and no wars breaking out and no way of making a name for himself that he could see. Now that is the way boys is always thinking, but he was the first one I ever heard come out and say it.

So then he set to work to get up a plan to make him celebrated, and pretty soon he struck it, and offered to take me and Jim in. Tom Sawyer was always free and generous that way. There's plenty of boys that's mighty good and friendly when *you've* got a good thing, but when a good thing happens to come their way they don't say a word to you and try to hog it all. That warn't ever Tom Sawyer's style, I can say that for him. There's plenty of boys that will come hankering and gruvveling around when you've got an apple and beg the core off of you, but when *they've* got one and you beg for the core and remind them how you give them a core one time, they make a mouth at you and say thank you most to death but there ain't a-going to *be* no core. But I notice they always git come up with; all you got to do is to wait. Jake Hooker always done that way, and it warn't two years till he got drownded.

Well, we went out in the woods on the hill, and Tom told us what it was. It was a Crusade.

"What's a crusade?" I says.

He looked scornful, the way he always done when he was ashamed of a person, and says—

"Huck Finn, do you mean to tell me you don't know what a crusade is?"

"No," says I, "I don't. And I don't care, nuther. I've lived till now and done without it, and had my health, too. But as soon as you tell me, I'll know, and that's soon enough. I don't see no use in finding out things and clogging my head up with them when I mayn't ever have any occasion for them. There was Lance Williams, he learnt how to talk Choctaw, and there warn't ever a Choctaw here till one come along and dug his grave for him. Now, then, what's a Crusade? But I can tell you one thing before you begin; if it's a patent right, there ain't no money in it. Bill Thompson, he—"

"Patent right!" he says. "I never see such an idiot. Why, a crusade is a kind of a war."

I thought he must be losing his mind. But no, he was in real earnest, and went right on, perfectly cam:

"A crusade is a war to recover the Holy Land from the paynim."

"Which Holy Land?"

"Why, *the* Holy Land—there ain't but one."

"What do *we* want of it?"

"Why, can't you understand? It's in the hands of the paynim, and it's our duty to take it away from them."

"WE WENT OUT IN THE WOODS ON THE HILL, AND TOM TOLD US WHAT
IT WAS. IT WAS A CRUSADE."

"How did we come to let them git holt of it?"

"We didn't come to let them git hold of it. They always had it."

"Why, Tom, then it must belong to them, don't it?"

"Why of course it does. Who said it didn't?"

I studied over it, but couldn't seem to git at the rights of it no way. I says—

"It's too many for me, Tom Sawyer. If I had a farm, and it was mine, and another person wanted it, would it be right for him to—"

"Oh, shucks! you don't know enough to come in when it rains, Huck Finn. It ain't a farm, it's entirely different. You see, it's like this. They own the land, just the mere land, and that's all they *do* own; but it was our folks, our Jews and Christians, that made it holy, and so they haven't any business to be there defiling it. It's a shame, and we oughtn't to stand it a minute. We ought to march against them and take it away from them."

"Why, it does seem to me it's the most mixed-up thing I ever see. Now if I had a farm, and another person—"

"Don't I tell you it hasn't got anything to *do* with farming? Farming is business; just common low-down worldly business, that's all it is, it's all you can say for it; but this is higher, this is religious, and totally different."

"Religious to go and take the land away from the people that owns it?"

"Certainly; it's always been considered so."

Jim he shook his head and says—

"Mars Tom, I reckon dey's a mistake 'bout it somers—dey mos' sholy is. I's religious mysef; en I knows plenty religious people, but I hain't run acrost none dat acts like dat."

It made Tom hot, and he says—

"Well, it's enough to make a body sick, such mullet-headed ignorance. If either of you knowed anything about history, you'd know that Richard Cur de Lyon, and the Pope, and Godfrey de Bulloyn, and lots more of the most noble-hearted and pious people in the world hacked and hammered at the paynims for more than two hundred years trying to take their land away from them and swum neck deep in blood the whole time—and yet here's a couple of sap-headed country yahoos out in the backwoods of Missouri setting themselves up to know more about the rights and the wrongs of it than they did! Talk about cheek!"

Well, of course that put a more different light on it, and me and Jim felt pretty cheap and ignorant, and wished we hadn't been quite so chipper. I couldn't say nothing, and Jim he couldn't for a while; then he says—

"Well, den, I reckon it's all right, becaze ef *dey* didn't know, dey ain' no use for po' ignorant folks like us to be tryin' to know; en so ef it's our duty we got to go en tackle it en do de bes' we kin. Same time, I feel as sorry for dem paynims as—Mars Tom, de hard part gwyne to be to kill folks dat a body hain't 'quainted wid and hain't done him no harm. Dat's it, you see. Ef we uz to go 'mongst 'em, jist us three, and say we's hungry, en ast 'em for a bite to eat, why maybe dey's jist like yuther people en niggers, don't you reckon dey is? Why, *dey'd* give it, I know dey would; en den—"

"Then what?"

"Well, Mars Tom, my idea is like dis. It ain't no use, we *can't* kill dem po' strangers dat ain't doin' us no harm, till we've had practice— I knows it perfectly well, Mars Tom, 'deed I knows it perfectly well. But ef we takes a axe or two, jist you en me en Huck, en slips acrost de river to-night arter de moon's gone down, en kills dat sick fambly dat's over on de Sny, en burns dey house down, en—"

"Oh, shut your head! you make me tired. I don't want to argue no more with people like you and Huck Finn, that's always wandering from the subject and ain't got any more sense than to try to reason out a thing that's pure theology by the laws that protects real estate."

Now that's just where Tom Sawyer warn't fair. Jim didn't mean no harm, and I didn't mean no harm. We knowed well enough that he was right and we was wrong, and all we was after was to get at the *how* of it, that was all; and the only reason he couldn't explain it so we could understand it was because we was ignorant—yes, and pretty dull, too, I ain't denying that; but land! that ain't no crime, I should think.

But he wouldn't hear no more about it; just said if we had tackled the thing in a proper spirit he would a raised a couple of thousand knights, and put them up in steel armor from head to heel and made me a lieutenant and Jim a sutler, and took the command himself and brushed the whole paynim outfit into the sea like flies and come back across the world in a glory like sunset. But he said we didn't know enough to take the chance when we had it, and he wouldn't

ever offer it again. And he didn't. When he once got set, you couldn't
budge him.

But I didn't care much. I am peaceable, and don't get up no rows
with people that ain't doing nothing to me. I allowed if the paynims
was satisfied I was, and we would let it stand at that.

Now Tom he got all that wild notion out of Walter Scott's books,
which he was always reading. And it *was* a wild notion, because in
my opinion he never could a raised the men, and if he did, as like
as not he would a got licked. I took the books and read all about it,
and as near as I could make out, most of the folks that shook farming
to go crusading had a mighty rocky time of it.

"HE WOULD A RAISED A COUPLE OF
THOUSAND KNIGHTS AND BRUSHED THE
WHOLE PAYNIM OUTFIT INTO THE SEA."

CHAPTER 2

Well Tom got up one thing after another, but they all had sore places in them somewheres and he had to shove them aside. So at last he was most about in despair. Then the St. Louis papers begun to talk a good deal about the balloon that was going to sail to Europe, and Tom sort of thought he wanted to go down and see what it looked like, but couldn't make up his mind. But the papers went on talking, and so he allowed that maybe if he didn't go he mightn't ever have another chance to see a balloon; and next, he found out that Nat Parsons was going down to see it, and that decided him of course. He wasn't going to have Nat Parsons coming back bragging about seeing the balloon and him having to listen to it and keep his head shut. So he wanted me and Jim to go, too, and we went.

It was a noble big balloon, and had wings, and fans, and all sorts of things, and wasn't like any balloon that is in the pictures. It was away out towards the edge of town in a vacant lot corner of Twelfth street, and there was a big crowd around it making fun of it and making fun of the man, which was a lean, pale feller with that soft kind of moonlight in his eyes, you know, and they kept saying it wouldn't go. It made him hot to hear them, and he would turn on them and shake his fist and say they was animals and blind, but some day they would find they'd stood face to face with one of the men that lifts up nations and makes civilizations, and was too dull to know it, and right here on this spot their own children and grandchildren would build a monument to him that would last a thousand years but his name would outlast the monument; and then the crowd would bust out in a laugh again and yell at him and ask him what was his name before he was married, and what he would take to don't, and what was his sister's cat's grandmother's name, and all them kinds of things that a crowd says when they've got hold of a feller they see they can plague. Well, the things they said *was* funny, yes, and mighty witty too, I ain't denying that, but all the same it warn't fair nor brave, all them people pitching on one, and they so glib and sharp, and him without any gift of talk to answer back with. But good land! what did he *want* to sass back for? You see it couldn't do him no good, and it was just nuts for them. They *had* him, you know. But that was his way; I reckon he couldn't help it; he was made so, I judge. He was a good enough sort of a cretur, and hadn't no harm in him, and was just a genius, as the papers said, which wasn't his fault, we can't all be sound, we've got to be the way we are made. As near as I can make out, geniuses think they know it all, and so they won't take people's advice, but always go their own way, which makes everybody forsake them and despise them, and that is perfectly natural. If they was humbler, and listened and tried to learn, it would be better for them.

The part the Professor was in was like a boat, and was big and roomy and had water-tight lockers around the inside to keep all sorts of things in, and a body could set on them and make beds on them, too. We went aboard, and there was twenty people there, snooping around and examining, and old Nat Parsons was there, too. The Professor kept fussing around getting ready, and the people went ashore, drifting out one at a time, and old Nat he was the last. Of course it wouldn't do to let him go out behind *us*. We mustn't budge till he was gone, so we could be last ourselves.

But he was gone, now, so it was time for us to follow. I heard a big shout, and turned around—the city was dropping from under us like a shot! It made me sick all through, I was so scared. Jim turned gray, and couldn't say a word, and Tom didn't say nothing, but looked excited. The city went on dropping, down, and down, and down, but we didn't seem to do nothing but hang in the air and stand still. The houses got smaller and smaller, and the city pulled itself together closer and closer, and the men and wagons got to looking like ants and bugs crawling around, and the streets was like cracks and threads; and then it all kind of melted together and there wasn't any city any more, it was only a big scab on the earth, and it seemed to me a body could see up the river and down the river about a thousand miles, though of course it wasn't so much. By and by the earth was a ball—just a round ball, of a dull color, with shiny stripes wriggling and winding around over it which was rivers. And the weather

was getting pretty chilly. The widder Douglas always told me the
world was round like a ball, but I never took no stock in a lot of them
superstitions o' hern, and of course I never paid no attention to that
one, because I could see, myself, that the world was the shape of a
plate, and flat. I used to go up on the hill and take a look all around
and prove it for myself, because I reckon the best way to get a sure
thing on a fact is to go and examine for yourself and not take it on
anybody's say-so. But I had to give in, now, that the widder was right.
That is, she was right as to the rest of the world, but she warn't right
about the part our village is in: that part is the shape of a plate, and
flat, I take my oath.

The Professor was standing still all this time like he was asleep, but
he broke loose, now, and he was mighty bitter. He says something
like this:

"Idiots! they said it wouldn't go. And they wanted to examine it
and spy around and get the secret of it out of me. But I beat them.
Nobody knows the secret but me. Nobody knows what makes it
move but me—and it's a new power! A new power, and a thousand
times the strongest in the earth. Steam's foolishness to it. They said I
couldn't go to Europe. To Europe! why, there's power aboard to last
five years, and food for three months; they are fools, what do *they*
know about it? Yes, and they said my air-ship was flimsy—why, she's
good for fifty years. I can sail the skies all my life if I want to, and
steer where I please, though they laughed at that, and said I couldn't.
Couldn't steer! Come here, boy; we'll see. You press these buttons
as I tell you."

He made Tom steer the ship all about and every which way, and
learnt him the whole thing in nearly no time, and Tom said it was
perfectly easy. He made him fetch the ship down most to the earth,
and had him spin her along so close to the Illinois prairies that a body
could talk to the farmers and hear everything they said, perfectly
plain; and he flung out printed bills to them that told about the balloon and said it was going to Europe. Tom got so he could steer
straight for a tree till he got nearly to it and then dart up and skin
right along over the top of it. Yes, and he learnt Tom how to land her;
and he done it first rate, too, and set her down in the prairie as soft
as wool; but the minute we started to skip out, the Professor says,
"No you don't!" and shot her up into the air again. It was awful. I

begun to beg, and so did Jim; but it only give his temper a rise, and he begun to rage around and look wild out of his eyes, and I was scared of him.

Well, then he got onto his troubles again, and mourned and grumbled about the way he was treated, and couldn't seem to git over it, and especially people's saying his ship was flimsy. He scoffed at that, and at their saying she warn't simple and would be always getting out of order. Get out of order—that graveled him; he said she couldn't any more get out of order than the solar sister. He got worse and worse, and I never see a person take on so. It give me the cold shivers to see him, and so it did Jim. By and by he got to yelling and screaming, and then he swore the world shouldn't ever have his secret at all, now, it had treated him so mean. He said he would sail his balloon around the globe just to show what it could do, and then he would sink it in the sea, and sink us all along with it, too. Well, it was the awfulest fix to be in—and here was night coming on.

He give us something to eat, and made us go to the other end of the boat, and laid down on a locker where he could boss all the

"HE SAID HE WOULD SAIL HIS BALLOON AROUND THE GLOBE."

"AND HERE WAS NIGHT COMING ON."

works, and put his old pepper-box revolver under his head and said
anybody that come fooling around there trying to land her, he would
kill him.

We set scrunched up together, and thought considerable, but
didn't say nothing, only just a word once in a while when a body had
to say something or bust, we was *so* scared and worried. The night
dragged along slow and lonesome. We was pretty low down, and the
moonshine made everything soft and pretty, and the farm houses
looked snug and homeful, and we could hear the farm sounds, and
wished we could be down there, but laws! we just slipped along over
them like a ghost, and never left a track.

Away in the night, when all the sounds was late sounds, and the
air had a late feel, too, and a late smell—about a two o'clock feel, as

near as I could make out,—Tom said the Professor was so quiet this
long time he must be asleep, and we better—

"Better what?" I says, in a whisper, and feeling sick all over, because
I knowed what he was thinking about.

"Better slip back there and tie him and land the ship," he says.

I says—

"No, sir! Don't you budge, Tom Sawyer."

And Jim—well, Jim was kind of gasping, he was so scared. He
says—

"Oh, Mars Tom, don't! Ef you tetches him we's gone—we's gone,
sho'! I ain't gwyne anear him, not for nothin' in dis worl'. Mars Tom,
he's plum crazy."

Tom whispers and says—

"That's why we've got to do something. If he wasn't crazy I
wouldn't give shucks to be anywhere but here; you couldn't hire me
to get out, now that I've got used to this balloon and over the scare of
being cut loose from the solid ground, if he was in his right mind;
but it's no good politics sailing around like this with a person that's
out of his head and says he's going around the world and then drown
us all. We've got to do something, I tell you, and do it before he wakes
up, too, or we mayn't ever get another chance. Come!"

But it made us turn cold and creepy just to think of it, and we said
we wouldn't budge. So Tom was for slipping back there by himself to
see if he couldn't get at the steering gear and land the ship. We begged
and begged him not to, but it warn't no use; so he got down on his
hands and knees and begun to crawl an inch at a time, we a-holding
our breath and watching. After he got to the middle of the boat he
crept slower than ever, and it did seem like years to me. But at last we
see him get to the Professor's head and sort of raise up soft and look a
good spell in his face and listen. Then we see him begin to inch along
again towards the Professor's feet where the steering-buttons was.
Well, he got there all safe, and was reaching slow and steady towards
the buttons, but he knocked down something that made a noise, and
we see him slump flat and soft in the bottom and lay still. The Professor stirred, and says "What's that?" But everybody kept dead still and
quiet, and he begun to mutter and mumble and nestle, like a person
that's going to wake up, and I thought I was going to die I was so worried and scared.

Then a cloud come over the moon, and I most cried, I was so glad. She buried herself deeper and deeper in the cloud, and it got so dark we couldn't see Tom no more. Then it begun to sprinkle rain, and we could hear the Professor fussing at his ropes and things and abusing the weather. We was afraid every minute he would touch Tom, and then we would be goners and no help, but Tom was already on his way home, and when we felt his hands on our knees my breath stopped sudden and my heart fell down amongst my other works, because I couldn't tell in the dark but it might be the Professor, which I thought it *was.*

Dear! I was so glad to have him back that I was just as near happy as a person could be that was up in the air that way with a deranged man. You can't land a balloon in the dark, and so I hoped it would keep on raining, for I didn't want Tom to go meddling any more and make us so awful uncomfortable. Well, I got my wish. It drizzled and drizzled along the rest of the night, which wasn't long, though it did seem so; and at daybreak it cleared, and the world looked mighty soft and gray and pretty, and the forests and fields so good to see again, and the horses and cattle standing sober and thinking. Next, the sun come a-blazing up gay and splendid, and then we begun to feel rusty and stretchy, and first we knowed we was all asleep.

CHAPTER 3

W̲E WENT TO SLEEP about four o'clock and woke up about eight. The Professor was setting back there at his end looking glum. He pitched us some breakfast, but he told us not to come abaft the midship compass. That was about the middle of the boat. Well, when you are sharp set, and you eat and satisfy yourself, everything looks pretty different from what it done before. It makes a body feel pretty near comfortable, even when he is up in a balloon with a genius. We got to talking together.

There was one thing that kept bothering me, and by and by I says—

"Tom, didn't we start east?"

"Yes."

"How fast have we been going?"

"Well, you heard what the Professor said when he was raging around; sometimes, he said, we was making fifty miles an hour, sometimes ninety, sometimes a hundred—said that with a gale to help he could make three hundred any time, and said if he wanted the gale, and wanted it blowing the right direction, he only had to go up higher or down lower and find it."

"Well, then, it's just as I reckoned. The Professor lied."

"Why?"

"Because if we was going so fast we ought to be past Illinois, oughtn't we?"

"Certainly."

"Well, we ain't."

"What's the reason we ain't?"

"I know by the color. We're right over Illinois yet. And you can see for yourself that Indiana ain't in sight."

"I wonder what's the matter with you, Huck. You know by the color?"

"Yes—of course I do."

"What's the color got to do with it?"

"It's got everything to do with it. Illinois is green, Indiana is pink. You show me any pink down here if you can. No, sir, it's green."

"Indiana *pink*? Why, what a lie!"

"It ain't no lie; I've seen it on the map, and it's pink."

You never see a person so aggravated and disgusted. He says—

"Well, if I was such a numskull as you, Huck Finn, I would jump over. Seen it on the map! Huck Finn, did you reckon the States was the same color out doors that they are on the map?"

"Tom Sawyer, what's a map for? Ain't it to learn you facts?"

"Of course."

"Well, then, how is it going to do that if it tells lies?—that's what I want to know."

"Shucks, you muggins, it *don't* tell lies."

"It don't, don't it?"

"No, it don't."

"All right, then; if it don't, there ain't no two States the same color. You git around *that*, if you can, Tom Sawyer."

He see I *had* him, and Jim see it, too, and I tell you I felt pretty good, for Tom Sawyer was always a hard person to git ahead of. Jim slapped his leg and says—

"I tell *you*! dat's smart, dat's right down smart! Ain't no use, Mars Tom, he got you *dis* time, he done got you dis time, sho'!" He slapped his leg again, and says, "My *lan'* but it was a smart one!"

I never felt so good in my life; and yet *I* didn't know I was saying anything much till it was out. I was just mooning along, perfectly careless, and not expecting anything was going to happen, and never *thinking* of such a thing at all, when all of a sudden out it come. Why, it was just as much a surprise to me as it was to any of them. It was just the same way it is when a person is munching along on a hunk of corn pone and not thinking about anything, and all of a sudden bites onto a di'mond. Now all that *he* knows, first-off, is, that it's some kind of gravel he's bit onto, but he don't find out it's a di'mond till he gits it out and brushes off the sand and crumbs and one thing or another and has a look at it, and then he's surprised and glad. Yes, and proud, too; though when you come to look the thing straight in the eye he ain't entitled to as much credit as he would a been if he'd been *hunting* di'monds. You can see the difference easy,

if you think it over. You see, an accident, that way, ain't fairly as big
a thing as a thing that's done a purpose. Anybody could find that
di'mond in that corn-pone; but mind you, it's got to be somebody
that's got *that kind of corn-pone.* That's where that feller's credit
comes in, you see; and that's where mine comes in. I don't claim no
great things, I don't reckon I could a done it again, but I done it that
time, that's all I claim. And I hadn't no more idea I could do such a
thing and warn't any more thinking about it or trying to, than you be,
this minute. Why, I was just as cam, a body couldn't be any cammer,
and yet all of a sudden out it come. I've often thought of that time,
and I can remember just the way everything looked, same as if it
was only last week. I can see it all; beautiful rolling country with
woods and fields and lakes for hundreds and hundreds of miles all
around, and towns and villages scattered everywheres under us, here
and there and yonder, and the Professor mooning over a chart on his
little table, and Tom's cap flopping in the rigging where it was hung up
to dry, and one thing in particular was a bird right alongside, not ten
foot off, going our way and trying to keep up, but losing ground all the
time, and a railroad train doing the same, down there, sliding along
amongst the trees and farms, and pouring out a long cloud of black
smoke and now and then a little puff of white; and when the white
was gone so long you had most forgot it, you would hear a little faint
toot, and that was the whistle; and we left the bird and the train both
behind, *way* behind, and done it easy, too.

But Tom he was huffy, and said me and Jim was a couple of ignorant blatherskites, and then he says—

"Suppose there's a brown calf and a big brown dog, and an artist is
making a picture of them. What is the *main* thing that that artist has
got to do? He has got to paint them so you can tell 'em apart the minute
you look at them, hain't he? Of course. Well, then, do you want him to
go and paint *both* of them brown? Certainly you don't. He paints one
of them blue, and then you can't make no mistake. It's just the same
with the maps. That's why they make every State a different color; it
ain't to deceive you, it's to keep you from deceiving yourself."

But I couldn't see no argument about that, and neither could Jim.
Jim shook his head, and says—

"Why, Mars Tom, ef you knowed what chuckleheads dem painters
is, you'd wait a long time befo' you'd fetch one er *dem* in to back up

a fac'. I's gwyne to tell you—den you kin see for youseff. I see one er 'em a-paintin' away, one day, down in old Hank Wilson's back lot, en I went down to see, en he was paintin' dat ole brindle cow wid de near horn gone—you knows de one I means. En I ast him what's he paintin' her for, en he say when he git her painted de picture's wuth a hunderd dollars. Mars Tom, he could a got de *cow* fer fifteen, en I *tole* him so. Well, sah, ef you'll b'lieve me, he jes' shuck his head en went on a-dobbin'. Bless you, Mars Tom, *dey* don't know nothin'."

Tom he lost his temper; I notice a person most always does, that's got laid out in an argument. He told us to shut up and don't stir the slush in our skulls any more, hold still and let it cake, and maybe we'd feel better. Then he see a town clock away off down yonder, and he took up the glass and looked at it, and then looked at his silver turnip, and then at the clock, and then at the turnip again, and says—

"That's funny—that clock's near about an hour fast."

So he put up his turnip. Then he see another clock, and took a look, and it was an hour fast, too. That puzzled him.

"That's a mighty curious thing," he says; "I don't understand that."

Then he took the glass and hunted up another clock, and sure enough it was an hour fast, too. Then his eyes begun to spread and his breath to come out kind of gaspy like, and he says—

"Ger-reat Scott, it's the *longitude!*"

I says, considerable scared—

"Well, what's been and gone and happened now?"

"Why, the thing that's happened is, that this old bladder has slid over Illinois and Indiana and Ohio like nothing, and this is the east end of Pennsylvania or New York, or somewheres around there."

"Tom Sawyer, you don't mean it!"

"Yes, I do, and it's so, dead sure. We've covered about fifteen degrees of longitude since we left St. Louis yesterday afternoon, and them clocks are *right*. We've come close onto eight hundred mile."

I didn't believe it, but it made the cold streaks trickle down my back just the same. In my experience I knowed it wouldn't take much short of two weeks to do it down the Mississippi on a raft.

Jim was working his mind, and studying. Pretty soon he says—

"Mars Tom, did you say dem clocks uz right?"

"Yes, they're right."

"Ain't yo' watch right, too?"

"She's right for St. Louis, but she's an hour wrong for here."

"Mars Tom, is you tryin' to let on dat de time ain't de *same* every-wheres?"

"No, it ain't the same everywheres, by a long shot."

Jim he looked distressed, and says—

"It grieve me to hear you talk like dat, Mars Tom; I's right down 'shamed to hear you talk like dat, arter de way you's been raised. Yassir, it 'd break yo' aunt Polly's heart to hear you."

Tom was astonished. He looked Jim over, wondering, and didn't say nothing, and Jim he went on:

"Mars Tom, who put de people out yonder in St. Louis? De Lord done it. Who put de people here whah we is? De Lord done it. Ain' dey bofe His chillen? 'Cose dey is. *Well*, den! is He gwyne to *'scriminate* 'twix' 'em?"

"'Scrimminate! I never heard such ignorant rot. There ain't no discriminating about it. When He makes you and some more of His children black, and makes the rest of us white, what do you call that?"

Jim see the pint. He was stuck. He couldn't answer. Tom says—

"He does discriminate, you see, when He wants to—but this case *here* ain't no discrimination of His, it's man's. The Lord made the day, and He made the night; but He didn't invent the hours, and He didn't distribute them around—man done it."

"Mars Tom, is dat so? Man done it?"

"Certainly."

"Who tole him he could?"

"Nobody. He never asked."

Jim studied a minute, and says—

"Well, dat do beat me. I wouldn't a tuck no sich resk. But some people ain't scared o' nothin'. Dey bangs right ahead, *dey* don't care what happens. So den dey's allays an hour's diffunce everywhah, Mars Tom?"

"An hour? No! It's four minutes' difference for every degree—of longitude, you know. Fifteen of 'em's an hour, thirty of 'em's two hours, and so on. When it's one o'clock Tuesday morning in England, it's eight o'clock the night before, in New York."

Jim moved a little away along the locker, and you could see he was insulted. He kept shaking his head and muttering, and so I slid along to him and patted him on the leg and petted him up, and got him over the worst of his feelings, and then he says—

"Mars Tom talkin' sich talk as dat—Choosday in one place en

Monday in t'other, bofe in de same day! Huck, dis ain' no place to
joke—up here whah we is. Two days in one day! How you gwyne to
git two days inter one day—can't git two hours inter one hour, kin
you? can't git two niggers inter one nigger-skin, kin you? can't git two
gallons o' whisky inter a one-gallon jug, kin you? No, sir, 'twould
strain de jug. Yas, en even den you couldn't, I doan b'lieve. Why,
looky here, Huck, sposen de Choosday was New Year's—now den!
Is you gwyne to tell me it's dis year in one place en las' year in t'other,
bofe in de identical same minute? It's de beatenest rubbage—I can't
stan' it, I can't stan' to hear tell 'bout it." Then he begun to shiver
and turn gray, and Tom says—

"Now what's the matter? What's the trouble?"

Jim could hardly speak, but he says—

"Mars Tom, you ain't jokin', en it's so?"

"No, I'm not, and it is so."

Jim shivered again, and says—

"Den dat Monday could be de Las' Day, en day wouldn't be no Las'
Day in England en de dead wouldn't be called. We mustn't go over
dah, Mars Tom, please git him to turn back; I wants to be whah—"

All of a sudden we see something, and all jumped up, and forgot
everything and begun to gaze. Tom says—

"Ain't that the—" He catched his breath, then says: "It is, sure
as you live—it's the ocean!"

That made me and Jim catch our breath, too. Then we all stood
putrified but happy, for none of us had ever seen an ocean, or ever
expected to. Tom kept muttering—

"Atlantic Ocean—Atlantic. Land, don't it sound great! . . . . .
And that's it—and we are a-looking at it—we! My, it's just too splendid to believe!"

Then we see a big bank of black smoke; and when we got nearer,
it was a city, and a monster she was, too, with a thick fringe of ships
around one edge; and wondered if it was New York, and begun to jaw
and dispute about it, and first we knowed, it slid from under us and
went flying behind, and here we was, out over the very ocean itself,
and going like a cyclone. Then we woke up, I tell you!

We made a break aft, and raised a wail, and begun to beg the
Professor to take pity on us and turn back and land us and let us go
back to our folks, which would be so grieved and anxious about us,

and maybe die if anything happened to us, but he jerked out his pistol and motioned us back, and we went, but nobody will ever know how bad we felt.

The land was gone, all but a little streak, like a snake, away off on the edge of the water, and down under us was just ocean, ocean, ocean—millions of miles of it, heaving, and pitching and squirming, and white sprays blowing from the wave-tops, and only a few ships in sight, wallowing around and laying over, first on one side and then on t'other, and sticking their bows under and then their sterns; and before long there warn't no ships at all, and we had the sky and the whole ocean all to ourselves, and the roomiest place I ever see and the lonesomest.

CHAPTER 4

AND IT GOT LONESOMER and lonesomer. There was the big sky up there, empty and awful deep, and the ocean down there without a thing on it but just the waves. All around us was a ring, a perfectly round ring, where the sky and the water come together; yes, a monstrous big ring, it was, and we right in the dead centre of it. Plum in the centre. We was racing along like a prairie fire, but it never made any difference, we couldn't seem to git past that centre no way; I couldn't see that we ever gained an inch on that ring. It made a body feel creepy, it was so curious and unaccountable.

Well, everything was so awful still that we got to talking in a very low voice, and kept on getting creepier and lonesomer and less and less talky, till at last the talk run dry altogether and we just set there and "thunk," as Jim calls it, and never said a word, the longest time.

The Professor never stirred till the sun was overhead, then he stood up and put a kind of a triangle to his eye, and Tom said it was a sextant and he was taking the sun, to see whereabouts the balloon was. Then he ciphered a little, and looked in a book, and then he begun to carry on again. He said lots of wild things, and amongst others he said he would keep up this hundred-mile gait till the middle of to-morrow afternoon and then he'd land in London.

We said we would be humbly thankful.

He was turning away, but he whirled around when we said that, and give us a long look, of his blackest kind—one of the maliciousest and suspiciousest looks I ever see. Then he says—

"You want to leave me. Don't try to deny it."

We didn't know what to say, so we held in and didn't say nothing at all.

He went aft and set down, but he couldn't seem to git that thing out of his mind. Every now and then he would rip out something about it, and try to make us answer him, but we dasn't.

"THE PROFESSOR SAID HE WOULD KEEP UP THIS HUNDRED-MILE GAIT
TILL TO-MORROW."

It got lonesomer and lonesomer right along, and it did seem to me I couldn't stand it. It was still worse when night begun to come on. By and by Tom pinched me and whispers—

"Look!"

I took a glance aft and see the Professor taking a whet out of a bottle.

I didn't like the looks of that. By and by he took another drink, and
pretty soon he begun to sing. It was dark, now, and getting black and
stormy. He went on singing, wilder and wilder, and the thunder begun
to mutter and the wind to wheeze and moan amongst the ropes, and
altogether it was awful. It got so black we couldn't see him any more,

"YOU WANT TO LEAVE ME. DON'T TRY TO DENY IT."

and wished we couldn't hear him, but we could. Then he got still; but
he warn't still ten minutes till we got suspicious, and wished he would
start up his noise again, so we could tell where he was. By and by
there was a flash of lightning, and we see him start to get up, but he
was drunk, and staggered and fell down. We heard him scream out
in the dark—

"They don't want to go to England—all right, I'll change the course.
They want to leave me. Well, they shall—and *now*!"

I most died when he said that. Then he was still again; still so long I couldn't bear it, and it did seem to me the lightning wouldn't *ever* come again. But at last there was a blessed flash, and there he was, on his hands and knees, crawling, and not four foot from us. My, but his eyes was terrible. He made a lunge for Tom and says, "Overboard *you* go!" but it was already pitch dark again, and I couldn't see whether he got him or not, and Tom didn't make a sound.

There was another long, horrible wait, then there was a flash and I see Tom's head sink down, outside the boat and disappear. He was on the rope ladder that dangled down in the air from the gunnel. The Professor let off a shout and jumped for him, and straight off it was pitch dark again, and Jim groaned out, "Po' Mars Tom, he's a goner!" and made a jump for the Professor, but the Professor warn't there.

Then we heard a couple of terrible screams—and then another, not so loud, and then another that was way below, and you could only *just* hear it, and I hear Jim say, *"Po' Mars Tom!"*

Then it was awful still, and I reckon a person could a counted four hundred thousand before the next flash come. When it come I see Jim on his knees, with his arms on the locker and his face buried in them, and he was crying. Before I could look over the edge, it was all dark again, and I was kind of glad, because I didn't want to see. But when the next flash come I was watching, and down there I see somebody a-swinging in the wind on that ladder, and it was Tom!

"Come up!" I shouts, "Come up, Tom!"

His voice was so weak, and the wind roared so, I couldn't make out what he said, but I thought he asked was the Professor up there. I shouts,—

"No, he's down in the ocean! Come up! Can we help you?"

Of course, all this in the dark.

"Huck, who is you hollerin' at?"

"I'm hollering at Tom."

"Oh, Huck, how kin you act so, when you knows po' Mars Tom's"—then he let off an awful scream and flung his head and his arms back and let off another one; because there was a white glare just then, and he had raised up his face just in time to see Tom's, as white as snow, rise above the gunnel and look him right in the eye. He thought it was Tom's ghost, you see.

Tom clumb aboard, and when Jim found it *was* him and not his ghost, he hugged him and slobbered all over him, and called him all sorts of loving names, and carried on like he was gone crazy, he was so glad. Says I—

"What did you wait for, Tom? Why didn't you come up at first?"

"THE THUNDER BOOMED, AND THE LIGHTNING GLARED, AND THE WIND SCREAMED IN THE RIGGING."

"I dasn't, Huck. I knowed somebody plunged down past me, but I didn't know who it was, in the dark. It could a been you, it could a been Jim."

That was the way with Tom Sawyer—always sound. He warn't coming up till he knowed where the Professor was.

The storm let go, about this time, with all its might, and it was dreadful the way the thunder boomed and tore, and the lightning glared out, and the wind sung and screamed in the rigging and the rain come down. One second you couldn't see your hand before you, and the next you could count the threads in your coat sleeve, and see a whole wide desert of waves pitching and tossing, through a kind of veil of rain. A storm like that is the loveliest thing there is, but it ain't at its best when you are up in the sky and lost, and it's wet and lonesome and there's just been a death in the family.

We set there huddled up in the bow, and talked low about the poor Professor, and everybody was sorry for him, and sorry the world had made fun of him and treated him so harsh, when he was doing the best he could and hadn't a friend nor nobody to encourage him and keep him from brooding his mind away and going deranged. There was plenty of clothes and blankets and everything at the other end, but we thought we druther take the rain than go meddling back there; you see it would seem so crawly to be where it was warm yet, as you might say, from a dead man. Jim said he would soak till he was mush before he would go there and maybe run up against that ghost betwixt the flashes. He said it always made him sick to *see* a ghost, and he'd druther die than *feel* of one.

CHAPTER 5

W<small>E TRIED</small> to make some plans, but we couldn't come to no agreement. Me and Jim was for turning around and going back home, but Tom allowed that by the time daylight come, so we could see our way, we would be so far towards England that we might as well go there and come back in a ship and have the glory of saying we done it.

About midnight the storm quit and the moon come out and lit up the ocean, and then we begun to feel comfortable and drowsy; so we stretched out on the lockers and went to sleep, and never woke up again till sun-up. The sea was sparkling like di'monds, and it was nice weather, and pretty soon our things was all dry again.

We went aft to find some breakfast, and the first thing we noticed was that there was a dim light burning in a compass back there under a hood. Then Tom was disturbed. He says—

"You know what that means, easy enough. It means that somebody has got to stay on watch and steer this thing the same as he would a ship, or she'll wander around and go wherever the wind wants her to."

"Well," I says, "what's she been doing since—er—since we had the accident?"

"Wandering," he says, kind of troubled, "Wandering, without any doubt. She's in a wind, now, that's blowing her south of east. We don't know how long that's been going on, either."

So then he pinted her east, and said he would hold her there whilst we rousted out the breakfast. The Professor had laid in everything a body could want; he couldn't a been better fixed. There warn't no milk for the coffee, but there was water and everything else you could want, and a charcoal stove and the fixings for it, and pipes and cigars and matches; and wine and liquor, which warn't in our line; and books and maps and charts, and an accordion, and furs and blankets, and no end of rubbish, like glass beads and brass jewelry, which Tom said was a sure sign that he had an idea of visiting around amongst savages. There was money, too. Yes, the Professor was well enough fixed.

After breakfast Tom learned me and Jim how to steer, and divided all of us up into four-hour watches, turn and turn about; and when his watch was out I took his place, and he got out the Professor's paper and pens and wrote a letter home to his aunt Polly telling her everything that had happened to us, and dated it *"In the Welkin, approaching England,"* and folded it together and stuck it fast with a red wafer, and directed it, and wrote above the direction in big writing, *"From Tom Sawyer the Erronort,"* and said it would sweat old Nat Parsons the postmaster when it come along in the mail. I says—

"Tom Sawyer, this ain't no welkin, it's a balloon."

"Well, now, who *said* it was a welkin, smarty?"

"You've wrote it on the letter, anyway."

"What of it? That don't mean that the balloon's the welkin."

"Oh, I thought it did. Well, then, what *is* a welkin?"

I see in a minute he was stuck. He raked and scraped around in his mind, but he couldn't find nothing, so he had to say—

"*I* don't know, and nobody don't know. It's just a word. And it's a mighty good word, too. There ain't many that lays over it. I don't believe there's *any* that does."

"Shucks," I says, "but what does it *mean?*—that's the pint."

"*I* don't know what it means, I tell you. It's a word that people uses for—for—well, it's ornamental. They don't put ruffles on a shirt to help keep a person warm, do they?"

" 'Course they don't."

"But they put them *on,* don't they?"

"Yes."

"All right, then; that letter I wrote is a shirt, and the welkin's the ruffle on it."

I judged that that would gravel Jim, and it did. He says—

"Now, Mars Tom, it ain't no use to talk like dat, en moreover it's sinful. *You* knows a letter ain't no shirt, en dey ain't no ruffles on it, nuther. Dey ain't no place to put 'em on, you can't put 'em on, en dey wouldn't stay on ef you did."

"Oh, *do* shut up, and wait till something's started that you know something about."

"Why, Mars Tom, sholy you don't mean to say I don't know about shirts, when goodness knows I's toted home de washin' ever sence—"

"I tell you this hasn't got anything to *do* with shirts. I only—"

"Why, Mars Tom! You said, yo' own self, dat a letter—"

"Do you want to drive me crazy? Keep still. I only used it as a metaphor."

That word kind of bricked us up for a minute. Then Jim says, ruther timid, because he see Tom was getting pretty tetchy—

"Mars Tom, what is a metaphor?"

"A metaphor's a—well, it's a—a metaphor's an illustration." He see that *that* didn't git home; so he tried again. "When I say birds of a feather flocks together, it's a metaphorical way of saying—"

"But dey *don't*, Mars Tom. No, sir, 'deed dey don't. Dey ain't no feathers dat's more alike den a bluebird's en a jaybird's, but ef you waits tell you catches *dem* birds a-flockin' together, you'll—"

"Oh, *give* us a rest. You can't get the simplest little thing through your thick skull. Now, don't bother me any more."

Jim was satisfied to stop. He was dreadful pleased with himself for catching Tom out. The minute Tom begun to talk about birds I judged he was a goner, because Jim knowed more about birds than both of us put together. You see, he had killed hundreds and hundreds of them, and that's the way to find out about birds. That's the way the people does that writes books about birds, and loves them so that they'll go hungry and tired and take any amount of trouble to find a new bird and kill it. Their name is ornithologers, and I could a been an ornithologer myself, because I always loved birds and creatures; and I started out to learn how to be one, and I see a bird setting on a dead limb of a high tree, singing, with his head tilted back and his mouth open, and before I thought I fired, and his song stopped and he fell straight down from the limb, all limp like a rag, and I run and picked him up, and he was dead, and his body was warm in my hand, and his head rolled about, this way and that, like his neck was broke, and there was a white skin over his eyes, and one little drop of blood on the side of his head, and laws! I couldn't see nothing more for the tears; and I hain't ever murdered no creature since, that warn't doing me no harm, and I ain't going to.

But I was aggravated about that welkin. I wanted to know. I got the subject up again, and then Tom explained, the best he could. He said when a person made a big speech the newspapers said the shouts of the people made the welkin ring. He said they always said that, but none of them ever told what it was, so he allowed it just meant outdoors and up high. Well, that seemed sensible enough, so I was satisfied, and said so. That pleased Tom and put him in a good humor again, and he says—

"Well, it's all right, then, and we'll let bygones be bygones. I don't know for certain what a welkin is, but when we land in London we'll make it ring, anyway, and don't you forget it."

He said an Erronort was a person who sailed around in balloons; and said it was a mighty sight finer to be Tom Sawyer the Erronort than to be Tom Sawyer the Traveler, and would be heard of all around the world, if we pulled through all right, and so he wouldn't give shucks to be a Traveler, now.

Towards the middle of the afternoon we got everything ready to land, and we felt pretty good, too, and proud; and we kept watching with the glasses, like Clumbus discovering America. But we couldn't see nothing but ocean. The afternoon wasted out and the sun shut down, and still there warn't no land anywheres. We wondered what was the matter, but reckoned it would come out all right, so we went on steering east, but went up on a higher level so we wouldn't hit any steeples or mountains in the dark.

It was my watch till midnight, and then it was Jim's; but Tom stayed up, because he said ship captains done that when they was making the land, and didn't stand no regular watch.

Well, when daylight come, Jim give a shout, and we jumped up and looked over, and there was the land, sure enough; land all around, as far as you could see, and perfectly level and yaller. We didn't know how long we had been over it. There warn't no trees, nor hills, nor rocks, nor towns, and Tom and Jim had took it for the sea. They took it for the sea in a dead cam; but we was so high up, anyway, that if it had been the sea and rough, it would a looked smooth, all the same, in the night, that way.

We was all in a powerful excitement, now, and grabbed the glasses and hunted everywheres for London, but couldn't find hide nor hair of it, nor any other settlement. Nor any sign of a lake or a river, either. Tom was clean beat. He said it warn't his notion of England, he thought England looked like America, and always had that idea. So he said we better have breakfast, and then drop down and inquire

the quickest way to London. We cut the breakfast pretty short, we
was so impatient. As we slanted along down, the weather begun to
moderate, and pretty soon we shed our furs. But it kept *on* moderat-
ing, and in a precious little while it was most too moderate. Why, the
sweat begun to fairly bile out of us. We was close down, now, and just
blistering!

We settled down to within thirty foot of the land. That is, it was
land if sand is land; for this wasn't anything but pure sand. Tom
and me clumb down the ladder and took a run to stretch our legs,
and it felt amazing good; that is, the stretching did, but the sand
scorched our feet like hot embers. Next, we see somebody coming,
and started to meet him; but we heard Jim shout, and looked around,
and he was fairly dancing, and making signs, and yelling. We couldn't
make out what he said, but we was scared, anyway, and begun to heel
it back to the balloon. When we got close enough, we understood the
words, and they made me sick:

"Run! run fo' yo' life! hit's a lion, I kin see him thoo de glass! Run,
boys, do please heel it de bes' you kin, he's busted outen de menagerie
en dey ain't nobody to stop him!"

It made Tom fly, but it took the stiffening all out of my legs. I could
only just gasp along the way you do in a dream when there's a ghost
a-gaining on you.

Tom got to the ladder and shinned up it a piece and waited for me;

"RUN! RUN FO' YO' LIFE!"

and as soon as I got a foothold on it he shouted to Jim to soar away. But Jim had clean lost his head, and said he had forgot how. So Tom shinned along up and told me to follow, but the lion was arriving, fetching a most gashly roar with every lope, and my legs shook so I dasn't try to take one of them out of the rounds for fear the other one would give way under me.

But Tom was aboard by this time, and he started the balloon up, a little, and stopped it again as soon as the end of the ladder was ten or twelve foot above ground. And there was the lion, a-ripping around under me, and roaring, and springing up in the air at the ladder and only missing it about a quarter of an inch, it seemed to me. It was delicious to be out of his reach, perfectly delicious, and made me feel good and thankful all up one side; but I was hanging there helpless and couldn't climb, and that made me feel perfectly wretched and miserable all down the other. It is most seldom that a person feels so mixed, like that; and is not to be recommended, either.

Tom asked me what he better do, but I didn't know. He asked me if I could hold on whilst he sailed away to a safe place and left the lion behind. I said I could if he didn't go no higher than he was now, but if he went higher I would lose my head and fall, sure. So he said, "Take a good grip," and he started.

"Don't go so fast," I shouted, "it makes my head swim."

He had started like a lightning express. He slowed down, and we glided over the sand slower, but still in a kind of sickening way, for it *is* uncomfortable to see things gliding and sliding under you like that and not a sound.

But pretty soon there was plenty of sound, for the lion was catching up. His noise fetched others. You could see them coming on the lope from every direction, and pretty soon there was a couple of dozen of them under me skipping up at the ladder and snarling and snapping at each other; and so we went skimming along over the sand, and these fellers doing what they could to help us to not forget the occasion; and then some tigers come, without an invite, and they started a regular riot down there.

We see this plan was a mistake. We couldn't ever git away from them at this gait, and I couldn't hold on forever. So Tom took a think and struck another idea. That was, to kill a lion with the pepper-box revolver and then sail away while the others stopped to fight over the

"SKIPPING UP AT THE LADDER AND SNARLING AND SNAPPING AT EACH OTHER."

carcase. So he stopped the balloon still, and done it, and then we sailed off while the fuss was going on, and come down a quarter of a mile off, and they helped me aboard; but by the time we was out of reach again, that gang was on hand once more. And when they see we was really gone and they couldn't get us, they set down on their hams and looked up at us so kind of disappointed that it was as much as a person could do not to see *their* side of the matter.

CHAPTER 6

I WAS SO WEAK that the only thing I wanted was a chance to lay down, so I made straight for my locker-bunk and stretched myself out there. But a body couldn't git back his strength in no such oven as that, so Tom give the command to soar, and Jim started her aloft. And mind you, it was a considerable strain on that balloon to lift the fleas, and reminded Tom of Mary had a little lamb its fleas was white as snow, but these wasn't; these was the dark-complected kind, the kind that's always hungry and ain't particular, and will eat pie when they can't git Christian. Wherever there's sand, you are a-going to find that bird; and the more sand the bigger the flock. Here it was all sand, and the result was according. I never see such a turnout.

We had to go up a mile before we struck comfortable weather; and we had to go up another mile before we got rid of them creturs; but when they begun to freeze, they skipped overboard. Then we come down a mile again where it was breezy and pleasant and just right, and pretty soon I was all straight again. Tom had been setting quiet and thinking; but now he jumps up and says—

"I bet you a thousand to one I know where we are. We're in the Great Sahara, as sure as guns!"

He was so excited he couldn't hold still. But I wasn't; I says—

"Well, then, where's the Great Sahara? In England, or in Scotland?"

"'Tain't in either, it's in Africa."

Jim's eyes bugged out, and he begun to stare down with no end of interest, because that was where his originals come from; but I didn't more than half believe it. I couldn't, you know; it seemed too awful far away for us to have traveled.

But Tom was full of his discovery, as he called it, and said the lions and the sand meant the Great Desert, sure. He said he could a found out, before we sighted land, that we was crowding the land somewheres, if he had thought of one thing; and when we asked him what, he said—

"These clocks. They're chronometers. You always read about them in sea-voyages. One of them is keeping Grinnage time, and the other one is keeping St. Louis time, like my watch. When we left St. Louis, it was four in the afternoon by my watch and this clock, and it was ten at night by this Grinnage clock. Well, at this time of the year the sun sets about seven o'clock. Now I noticed the time yesterday evening when the sun went down, and it was half past five o'clock by the Grinnage clock, and half past eleven, a.m., by my watch and the other clock. You see, the sun rose and set by my watch in St. Louis, and the Grinnage clock was six hours fast; but we've come so far east that it comes within less than an hour and a half of setting by the Grinnage clock, now, and I'm away out—more than four hours and a half out. You see, that meant that we was closing up on the longitude of Ireland, and would strike it before long if we was pinted right—which we wasn't. No, sir, we've been a-wandering—wandering way-down south of east, and it's my opinion we are in Africa. Look at this map. You see how the shoulder of Africa sticks out to the west. Think how fast we've traveled; if we had gone straight east we would be long past England by this time. You watch for noon, all of you, and we'll stand up, and when we can't cast a shadow we'll find that this Grinnage clock is coming mighty close to marking twelve. Yes, sir, I think we're in Africa; and it's just bully."

Jim was gazing down with the glass. He shook his head and says—

"Mars Tom, I reckon dey's a mistake somers, I hain't seen no niggers, yit."

"That's nothing; they don't live in the Desert. What is that, way off yonder? Gimme a glass."

He took a long look, and said it was like a black string stretched across the sand, but he couldn't guess what it was.

"Well," I says, "I reckon maybe you've got a chance, now, to find out whereabouts this balloon is, because as like as not that is one of these lines here, that's on the map, that you call meridians of longitude, and we can drop down and look at its number, and—"

"Oh, shucks, Huck Finn, I never see such a lunkhead as you. Did you s'pose there's meridians of longitude on the *earth*?"

"Tom Sawyer, they're set down on the map, and you know it perfectly well, and here they are, and you can see for yourself."

"Of course they're on the map, but that's nothing; there ain't any on the *ground*."

"Tom, do you know that to be so?"

"Certainly I do."

"Well, then, that map's a liar again. I never see such a liar as that map."

He fired up at that, and I was ready for him, and Jim was warming up his opinion, too, and the next minute we'd a broke loose on another argument, if Tom hadn't dropped the glass and begun to clap his hands like a maniac and sing out—

"Camels!—camels!"

So I grabbed a glass, and Jim, too, and took a look, but I was disappointed, and says—

"Camels your granny, they're spiders."

"Spiders in a desert, you shad? Spiders walking in a procession? You don't ever reflect, Huck Finn, and I reckon you really haven't got anything to reflect *with*. Don't you know we're as much as a mile up in the air, and that that string of crawlers is two or three miles away? Spiders, good land! Spiders as big as a cow? P'raps you'd like to go down and milk one of 'em. But they're camels, just the same. It's a caravan, that's what it is, and it's a mile long."

"Well, then, le's go down and look at it. I don't believe in it, and ain't going to till I see it and know it."

"All right," he says, and give the command: "Lower away."

As we come slanting down into the hot weather, we could see that it was camels, sure enough, plodding along, an everlasting string of them, with bales strapped to them, and several hundred men, in long white robes, and a thing like a shawl bound over their heads and hanging down with tassels and fringes; and some of the men had long guns and some hadn't, and some was riding and some was walking. And the weather—well it was just roasting. And how slow they did creep along! We swooped down, now, all of a sudden, and stopped about a hundred yards over their heads.

The men all set up a yell, and some of them fell flat on their stomachs, some begun to fire their guns at us, and the rest broke and scampered every which way, and so did the camels.

We see that we was making trouble, so we went up again about a mile, to the cool weather, and watched them from there. It took them an hour to get together and form the procession again; then they started along, but we could see by the glasses that they wasn't paying much attention to anything but us. We poked along, looking down at

"WE SWOOPED DOWN, NOW, ALL OF A SUDDEN."

them with the glasses, and by and by we see a big sand mound, and
something like people the other side of it, and there was something
like a man laying on top of the mound, that raised his head up every
now and then, and seemed to be watching the caravan or us, we didn't

know which. As the caravan got nearer, he sneaked down on the other side and rushed to the other men and horses—for that is what they was—and we see them mount in a hurry; and next, here they come, like a house afire, some with lances and some with long guns, and all of them yelling the best they could.

They come a-tearing down onto the caravan, and the next minute both sides crashed together and was all mixed up, and there was such another popping of guns as you never heard, and the air got so full of smoke you could only catch glimpses of them struggling together. There must a been six hundred men in that battle, and it was terrible to see. Then they broke up into gangs and groups, fighting, tooth and nail, and scurrying and scampering around, and laying into each other like everything; and whenever the smoke cleared a little you could see dead and wounded people and camels scattered far and wide and all about, and camels racing off in every direction.

At last the robbers see they couldn't win, so their chief sounded a signal, and all that was left of them broke away and went scampering across the plain. The last man to go snatched up a child and carried it off in front of him on his horse, and a woman run screaming and begging after him, and followed him away off across the plain till she was separated a long ways from her people; but it warn't no use, and she had to give it up, and we see her sink down on the sand and cover her face with her hands. Then Tom took the hellum, and started for that yahoo, and we come a-whizzing down and made a swoop, and knocked him out of the saddle, child and all; and he was jarred considerable, but the child wasn't hurt, but laid there working its hands and legs in the air like a tumble-bug that's on its back and can't turn over. The man went staggering off to overtake his horse, and didn't know what had hit him, for we was three or four hundred yards up in the air by this time.

We judged the woman would go and get the child, now, but she didn't. We could see her, through the glass, still setting there, with her head bowed down on her knees; so of course she hadn't seen the performance, and thought her child was clean gone with the man. She was nearly a half a mile from her people, so we thought we might go down to the child, which was about a quarter of a mile beyond her, and snake it to her before the caravan people could git to us to do us any harm; and besides, we reckoned they had enough business on

"THE LAST MAN TO GO SNATCHED UP A CHILD AND CARRIED IT OFF
IN FRONT OF HIM ON HIS HORSE."

their hands for one while, anyway, with the wounded. We thought
we'd chance it, and we did. We swooped down and stopped, and Jim
shinned down the ladder and fetched up the cub, which was a nice
fat little thing, and in a noble good humor, too, considering it was just
out of a battle and been tumbled off of a horse; and then we started
for the mother, and stopped back of her and tolerable near by, and

Jim slipped down and crept up easy, and when he was close back of her the child goo-goo'd, the way a child does, and she heard it, and whirled and fetched a shriek of joy, and made a jump for the kid and snatched it and hugged it, and dropped it and hugged Jim, and then snatched off a gold chain and hung it around Jim's neck, and hugged him again, and jerked up the child again and mashed it to her breast, a-sobbing and glorifying all the time, and Jim he shoved for the ladder and up it and in a minute we was back up in the sky and the woman was staring up, with the back of her head between her shoulders and the child with its arms locked around her neck. And there she stood, as long as we was in sight a-sailing away in the sky.

"WE COME A-WHIZZING DOWN AND MADE A SWOOP, AND KNOCKED HIM
OUT OF THE SADDLE, CHILD AND ALL."

CHAPTER 7

Noon!" SAYS TOM, and so it was. His shadder was just a blot around his feet. We looked, and the Grinnage clock was so close to twelve the difference didn't amount to nothing. So Tom said London was right north of us or right south of us, one or t'other, and he reckoned by the weather and the sand and the camels it was north; and a good many miles north, too; as many as from New York to the city of Mexico, he guessed.

Jim said he reckoned a balloon was a good deal the fastest thing in the world, unless it might be some kinds of birds—a wild pigeon, maybe, or a railroad.

But Tom said he had read about railroads in England going nearly a hundred miles an hour for a little ways, and there never was a bird in the world that could do that—except one, and that was a flea.

"A flea? Why, Mars Tom, in de fust place he ain't a bird, strickly speakin'—"

"He ain't a bird, ain't he? Well, then, what is he?"

"I don't rightly know, Mars Tom, but I speck he's only jist a animal. No, I reckon dat won't do, nuther, he ain't big enough for a animal. He mus' be a bug. Yassir, dat's what he is, he's a bug."

"I bet he ain't, but let it go. What's your second place?"

"Well, in de second place, birds is creturs dat goes a long ways, but a flea don't."

"He don't, don't he? Come, now, what *is* a long distance, if you know?"

"Why, it's miles, en lots of 'em—anybody knows dat."

"Can't a man walk miles?"

"Yassir, he kin."

"As many as a railroad?"

"Yassir, if you give him time."

"Can't a flea?"

"Well,—I s'pose so—ef you gives him heaps of time."

"Now you begin to see, don't you, that *distance* ain't the thing to judge by, at all; it's the time it takes to go the distance *in*, that *counts*, ain't it?"

"Well, hit do look sorter so, but I wouldn't a b'lieved it, Mars Tom."

"It's a matter of *proportion*, that's what it is; and when you come to gage a thing's speed by its size, where's your bird and your man and your railroad, alongside of a flea? The fastest man can't run more

"AND WHERE'S YOUR RAILROAD, 'LONGSIDE OF A FLEA?"

than about ten miles in an hour—not much over ten thousand times his own length. But all the books says any common ordinary third-class flea can jump a hundred and fifty times his own length; yes, and he can make five jumps a second, too,—seven hundred and fifty times his own length, in one little second—for he don't fool away any time stopping and starting—he does them both at the same time; you'll see, if you try to put your finger on him. Now that's a common ordinary third-class flea's gait; but you take an Eyetalian *first*-class,

that's been the pet of the nobility all his life and hasn't ever knowed
what want or sickness or exposure was, and he can jump more than
three hundred times his own length, and keep it up all day, five such
jumps every second, which is fifteen hundred times his own length.
Well, suppose a man could go fifteen hundred times his own length
in a second—say, a mile and a half? It's ninety miles a minute; it's
considerable more than five thousand miles an hour. Where's your
man, now?—yes, and your bird, and your railroad, and your balloon?

"WHERE'S YOUR MAN, NOW?"

Laws, they don't amount to shucks 'longside of a flea. A flea is just a
comet biled down small."

Jim was a good deal astonished, and so was I. Jim said—

"Is dem figgers jist edjackly true, en no jokin' en no lies, Mars
Tom?"

"Yes, they are; they're perfectly true."

"Well, den, honey, a body's got to respec' a flea. I ain't had no
respec' for um befo', scasely, but dey ain' no gittin' roun' it, dey do
deserve it, dat's certain."

"Well, I bet they do. They've got ever so much more sense, and
brains, and brightness, in proportion to their size, than any other
cretur in the world. A person can learn them most anything; and they
learn it quicker than any other cretur, too. They've been learnt to

haul little carriages in harness, and go this way and that way and t'other way according to orders; yes, and to march and drill like soldiers, doing it as exact, according to orders, as soldiers does it. They've been learnt to do all sorts of hard and troublesome things. S'pose you could cultivate a flea up to the size of a man, and keep his natural smartness a-growing and a-growing right along up, bigger and bigger, and keener and keener, in the same proportion—where'd the human race be, do you reckon? That flea would be President of the United States, and you couldn't any more prevent it than you can prevent lightning."

"My lan', Mars Tom, I never knowed dey was so much *to* de beas'. No, sir, I never had no idea of it, and dat's de fac'."

"There's more to him, by a long sight, than there is to any other cretur, man or beast, in proportion to size. He's the interestingest of them all. People have so much to say about an ant's strength, and an elephant's, and a locomotive's. Shucks, they don't begin with a flea. He can lift two or three hundred times his own weight. And none of them can come anywhere near it. And moreover, he has got notions of his own, and is very particular, and you can't fool him; his instinct,

"THAT FLEA WOULD BE PRESIDENT OF THE UNITED STATES,
AND YOU COULDN'T PREVENT IT."

or his judgment, or whatever it is, is perfectly sound and clear, and
don't ever make a mistake. People think all humans are alike to a flea.
It ain't so. There's folks that he won't go anear, hungry or not hungry,
and I'm one of them. I've never had one of them on me in my life."

"Mars Tom!"

"It's so; I ain't joking."

"Well, sah, I hain't ever heard de likes er dat, befo'."

Jim couldn't believe it, and I couldn't; so we had to drop down to
the sand and git a supply, and see. Tom was right. They went for me
and Jim by the thousand, but not a one of them lit on Tom. There
warn't no explaining it, but there it was, and there warn't no getting
around it. He said it had always been just so, and he'd just as soon be
where there was a million of them as not, they'd never touch him
nor bother him.

We went up to the cold weather for a freeze-out, and stayed a little
spell, and then come back to the comfortable weather and went lazy-
ing along twenty or twenty-five mile an hour, the way we'd been
doing for the last few hours. The reason was, that the longer we was
in that solemn, peaceful Desert, the more the hurry and fuss got kind
of soothed down in us, and the more happier and contented and
satisfied we got to feeling, and the more we got to liking the Desert,
and then loving it. So we had cramped the speed down, as I was saying,
and was having a most noble good lazy time, sometimes watching
through the glasses, sometimes stretched out on the lockers reading,
sometimes taking a nap.

It didn't seem like we was the same lot that was in such a sweat to
find land and git ashore, but it was. But we had got over that—clean
over it. We was used to the balloon, now, and not afraid any more, and
didn't want to be anywheres else. Why, it seemed just like home; it
most seemed as if I had been born and raised in it, and Jim and Tom
said the same. And always I had had hateful people around me,
a-nagging at me, and pestering of me, and scolding, and finding fault,
and fussing and bothering, and sticking to me, and keeping after me,
and making me do this, and making me do that and t'other, and
always selecting out the things I didn't want to do, and then giving me
Sam Hill because I shirked and done something else, and just aggra-
vating the life out of a body all the time; but up here in the sky it was
so still, and sunshiny and lovely, and plenty to eat, and plenty of sleep,

and strange things to see, and no nagging and pestering, and no good people, and just holiday all the time. Land, I warn't in no hurry to git out and buck at civilization again. Now, one of the worst things about civilization is, that anybody that gits a letter with trouble in it comes and tells you all about it and makes you feel bad, and the newspapers fetches you the troubles of everybody all over the world, and keeps you down-hearted and dismal most all the time, and it's such a heavy load for a person. I hate them newspapers; and I hate letters; and if I had my way I wouldn't allow nobody to load his troubles onto other folks he ain't acquainted with, on t'other side of the world, that way. Well, up in a balloon there ain't any of that, and it's the darlingest place there is.

We had supper, and that night was one of the prettiest nights I ever see. The moon made it just like daylight, only a heap softer; and once we see a lion standing all alone by himself, just all alone in the earth, it seemed like, and his shadder laid on the sand by him like a puddle of ink. That's the kind of moonlight to have.

Mainly we laid on our backs and talked, we didn't want to go to sleep. Tom said we was right in the midst of the Arabian Nights, now. He said it was right along here that one of the cutest things in that book happened; so we looked down and watched while he told about it, because there ain't anything that is so interesting to look at as a place that a book has talked about. It was a tale about a camel driver that had lost his camel, and he come along in the Desert and met a man, and says—

"Have you run across a stray camel to-day?"

And the man says—

"Was he blind in his left eye?"

"Yes."

"Had he lost an upper front tooth?"

"Yes."

"Was his off hind leg lame?"

"Yes."

"Was he loaded with millet seed on one side and honey on the other?"

"Yes, but you needn't go into no more details—that's the one, and I'm in a hurry. Where did you see him?"

"I hain't seen him at all," the man says.

"Hain't seen him at all? How can you describe him so close, then?"

"Because when a person knows how to use his eyes, everything he sees has got a meaning to it; but most people's eyes ain't any good to them. I knowed a camel had been along, because I seen his track. I knowed he was lame in his off hind leg because he had favored that foot and trod light on it and his track showed it. I knowed he was blind on his left side because he only nibbled the grass on the right side of the trail. I knowed he had lost an upper front tooth because where he bit into the sod his teeth-print showed it. The millet seed sifted out on one side—the ants told me that; the honey leaked out on the other—the flies told me that. I know all about your camel, but I hain't seen him."

Jim says—

"Go on, Mars Tom, hit's a mighty good tale, and powerful interestin'."

"That's all," Tom says.

"*All?*" says Jim, astonished. "What come o' de camel?"

"I don't know."

"Mars Tom, don't de tale say?"

"No."

Jim puzzled a minute, then he says—

"Well! ef dat ain't de beatenes' tale ever *I* struck. Jist gits to de place whah de intrust is gittin' red hot, en down she breaks. Why, Mars Tom, dey ain't no *sense* in a tale dat acts like dat. Hain't you got no *idea* whether de man got de camel back er not?"

"No, I haven't."

I see, myself, there warn't no sense in the tale, to chop square off, that way, before it come to anything, but I warn't going to say so, because I could see Tom was souring up pretty fast over the way it flatted out and the way Jim had popped onto the weak place in it, and I don't think it's fair for everybody to pile onto a feller when he's down. But Tom he whirls on me and says—

"What do *you* think of the tale?"

Of course, then, I had to come out and make a clean breast and say it did seem to me, too, same as it did to Jim, that as long as the tale stopped square in the middle and never got to no place, it really warn't worth the trouble of telling.

Tom's chin dropped on his breast, and 'stead of being mad, as I reckoned he'd be, to hear me scoff at his tale that way, he seemed to be only sad; and he says—

"Some people can see, and some can't—just as that man said. Let alone a camel, if a cyclone had gone by, *you* duffers wouldn't a noticed the track."

I don't know what he meant by that, and he didn't say; it was just one of his irrulevances, I reckon—he was full of them, sometimes, when he was in a close place and couldn't see no other way out—but I didn't mind. We'd spotted the soft place in that tale sharp enough, he couldn't git away from that little fact. It graveled him like the nation, too, I reckon, much as he tried not to let on.

CHAPTER 8

WE HAD AN EARLY breakfast in the morning, and set looking down on the Desert, and the weather was ever so bammy and lovely, although we warn't high up. You have to come down lower and lower after sundown, in the Desert, because it cools off so fast; and so, by the time it is getting towards dawn you are skimming along only a little ways above the sand.

We was watching the shadder of the balloon slide along the ground, and now and then gazing off across the Desert to see if anything was stirring, and then down at the shadder again, when all of a sudden almost right under us we see a lot of men and camels laying scattered about, perfectly quiet, like they was asleep.

We shut off the power, and backed up and stood over them, and then we see that they was all dead. It give us the cold shivers. And it made us hush down, too, and talk low, like people at a funeral. We dropped down slow, and stopped, and me and Tom clumb down and went amongst them. There was men, and women, and children. They was dried by the sun, and dark and shriveled and leathery, like the pictures of mummies you see in books. And yet they looked just as human, you wouldn't a believed it; just like they was asleep; some laying on their backs, with their arms spread on the sand, some on their sides, some on their faces, just as natural, though the teeth showed more than usual. Two or three was setting up. One was a woman, with her head bent over, and a child was laying across her lap. A man was setting with his hands locked around his knees, staring out of his dead eyes at a young girl that was stretched out before him. He looked so mournful, it was pitiful to see. And you never see a place so still as that was. He had straight black hair hanging down by his cheeks, and when a little faint breeze fanned it and made it wag, it made me shudder, because it seemed as if he was wagging his head.

Some of the people and animals was partly covered with sand, but most of them not, for the sand was thin there, and the bed was gravel, and hard. Most of the clothes had rotted away and left the bodies partly naked; and when you took hold of a rag, it tore with a touch, like spider-web. Tom reckoned they had been laying there for years.

Some of the men had rusty guns by them, some had swords on, and had shawl-belts with long silver-mounted pistols stuck in them. All the camels had their loads on, yet, but the packs had busted or rotted and spilt the freight out on the ground. We didn't reckon the swords was any good to the dead people any more, so we took one apiece, and some pistols. We took a small box, too, because it was so handsome and inlaid so fine; and then we wanted to bury the people; but there warn't no way to do it that we could think of, and nothing to do it with but sand, and that would blow away again, of course. We did start to cover up that poor girl, first laying some shawls from a busted bale on her; but when we was going to put sand on her, the man's hair wagged again and give us a shock, and we stopped, because it looked like he was trying to tell us he didn't want her covered up so he couldn't see her no more. I reckon she was dear to him, and he would a been so lonesome.

Then we mounted high and sailed away, and pretty soon that black spot on the sand was out of sight and we wouldn't ever see them poor people again in this world. We wondered, and reasoned, and tried to guess how they come to be there, and how it had all happened to them, but we couldn't make it out. First we thought maybe they got lost, and wandered around and about till their food and water give out and they starved to death; but Tom said no wild animals nor vultures hadn't meddled with them, and so that guess wouldn't do. So at last we give it up, and judged we wouldn't think about it no more, because it made us low spirited.

Then we opened the box, and it had gems and jewels in it, quite a pile, and some little veils of the kind the dead women had on, with fringes made out of curious gold money that we warn't acquainted with. We wondered if we better go and try to find them again and give it back; but Tom thought it over and said no, it was a country that was full of robbers, and they would come and steal it, and then the sin would be on us for putting the temptation in their way. So we went on; but I wished we had took all they had, so there wouldn't a been no temptation at all left.

We had had two hours of that blazing weather down there, and

"WE OPENED THE BOX, AND IT HAD GEMS AND JEWELS IN IT."

was dreadful thirsty when we got aboard again. We went straight for
the water, but it was spoiled and bitter, besides being pretty near hot
enough to scald your mouth. We couldn't drink it. It was Mississippi
river water, the best in the world, and we stirred up the mud in it
to see if that would help, but no, the mud wasn't any better than
the water.

Well, we hadn't been so very, very thirsty before, whilst we was
interested in the lost people, but we was, now, and as soon as we found
we couldn't have a drink, we was more than thirty-five times as
thirsty as we was a quarter of a minute before. Why, in a little while
we wanted to hold our mouths open and pant like a dog.

Tom said keep a sharp lookout, all around, everywheres, because
we'd got to find an oasis or there warn't no telling what would happen.
So we done it. We kept the glasses gliding around all the time, till our

arms got so tired we couldn't hold them any more. Two hours—three hours—just gazing and gazing, and nothing but sand, sand, *sand*, and you could see the quivery heat-shimmer playing over it. Dear, dear, a body don't know what real misery is till he is thirsty all the way through, and is certain he ain't ever going to come to any water any more. At last I couldn't stand it to look around on them baking plains; I laid down on the locker and give it up.

But by and by Tom raised a whoop, and there she was! A lake, wide and shiny, with pam trees leaning over it asleep, and their shadders in the water just as soft and delicate as ever you see. I never see anything look so good. It was a long ways off, but that warn't anything to us; we just slapped on a hundred-mile gait, and calculated to be there in seven minutes; but she stayed the same old distance away, all the time, we couldn't seem to gain on her; yes, sir, just as far, and shiny, and like a dream, but we couldn't get no nearer; and at last, all of a sudden, she was gone!

Tom's eyes took a spread, and he says—

"Boys, it was a *myridge*!"

Said it like he was glad. I didn't see nothing to be glad about. I says—

"Maybe. I don't care nothing about its name, the thing I want to know is, what's become of it?"

Jim was trembling all over, and so scared he couldn't speak, but he wanted to ask that question himself if he could a done it. Tom says—

"What's *become* of it? Why, you see, yourself, it's gone."

"Yes, I know; but where's it gone *to*?"

He looked me over and says—

"Well, now, Huck Finn, where *would* it go to? Don't you know what a myridge is?"

"No, I don't. What is it?"

"It ain't anything but imagination. There ain't anything *to* it."

It warmed me up a little to hear him talk like that, and I says—

"What's the use you talking that kind of stuff, Tom Sawyer? Didn't I see the lake?"

"Yes—you think you did."

"I don't think nothing about it, I *did* see it."

"I tell you you *didn't* see it, either—because it warn't there to see."

It astonished Jim to hear him talk so, and he broke in and says, kind of pleading and distressed—

"Mars Tom, *please* don't say sich things in sich an awful time as dis. You ain't only reskin' yo' own self, but you's reskin' us—same way like Anna Nias en Suffira. De lake *wuz* dah—I seen it jis as plain as I sees you en Huck dis minute."

I says—

"Why, he seen it himself! He was the very one that seen it first. *Now,* then!"

"Yes, Mars Tom, hit's so—you can't deny it. We all seen it, en dat *prove* it was dah."

"Proves it! *How* does it prove it?"

"Same way it does in de courts en everywheres, Mars Tom. One pusson might be drunk or dreamy or suthin', en he could be mistaken; en two might, maybe; but I tell you, sah, when three sees a thing, drunk er sober, it's *so.* Dey ain't no gittin' aroun' dat, en you knows it, Mars Tom."

"I don't know nothing of the kind. There used to be forty thousand million people that seen the sun move from one side of the sky to the other every day. Did that prove that the sun *done* it?"

" 'Course it did. En besides, dey warn't no 'casion to prove it. A body 'at's got any sense ain't gwyne to doubt it. Dah she is, now—a-sailin' thoo de sky des like she allays done."

Tom turned on me, then, and says—

"What do *you* say—is the sun standing still?"

"Tom Sawyer, what's the use to ask such a jackass question? Anybody that ain't blind can see it don't stand still."

"Well," he says, "I'm lost in the sky with no company but a passel of low-down animals that don't know no more than the head boss of a university did three or four hundred years ago. Why, blame it, Huck Finn, there was Popes, in them days, that knowed as much as *you* do."

It warn't fair play, and I let him know it. I says—

"Throwin' mud ain't arguin', Tom Sawyer."

"Who's throwin' mud?"

"You done it."

"I never. It ain't no disgrace, I reckon, to compare a backwoods Missouri muggins like you to a Pope, even the orneriest one that ever set on the throne. Why, it's an honor to you, you tadpole, the *Pope's*

the one that's hit hard, not *you*, and you couldn't blame him for
cussing about it, only they don't cuss. Not now they don't, I mean."

"Sho, Tom, did they ever?"

"In the Middle Ages? Why, it was their common diet."

"No! You don't really mean they cussed?"

That started his mill a-going and he ground out a regular speech,
the way he done sometimes when he was feeling his oats, and I got
him to write down some of the last half of it for me, because it was
like book-talk and tough to remember, and had words in it that I
warn't used to and is pretty tiresome to spell:

"Yes, they did. I don't mean that they went charging around the
way Ben Miller does, and put the cuss-words just the same way *he*
puts them. No, they used the same words, but they put them together
different, because they'd been learnt by the very best masters, and
they knowed *how*, which Ben Miller don't, because he just picked
it up, here and there and around, and hain't had no competent person
to learn him. But *they* knowed. It warn't no frivolous random cussing,
like Ben Miller's, that starts in anywheres and comes out nowheres,
it was scientific cussing, and systematic; and it was stern, and solemn,
and awful, not a thing for you to stand off and laugh at, the way
people does when that poor ignorant Ben Miller gits a-going. Why,
Ben Miller's kind can stand up and cuss a person a week, steady, and
it wouldn't phaze him no more than a goose cackling, but it was a
mighty different thing in them Middle Ages when a Pope, educated
to cuss, got his cussing-things together and begun to lay into a king,
or a kingdom, or a heretic, or a Jew, or anybody that was unsatisfac-
tory and needed straightening out. He didn't go at it harum-scarum;
no, he took that king or that other person, and begun at the top, and
cussed him all the way down in detail. He cussed him in the hairs
of his head, and in the bones of his skull, and in the hearing of his
ears, and in the sight of his eyes, and in the breath of his nostrils, and
in his vitals, and in his veins, and in his limbs and his feet and his
hands, and the blood and flesh and bones of his whole body; and
cussed him in the loves of his heart and in his friendships, and turned
him out in the world, and cussed anybody that give him food to eat,
or shelter and bed, or water to drink, or rags to cover him when he
was freezing. Land, *that* was cussing worth talking about; that was
the only cussing worth shucks that's ever been done in this world—

the man it fell on, or the country it fell on, would better a been dead,
forty times over. Ben Miller! The idea of him thinking *he* can cuss.
Why, the poorest little one-horse back-country bishop in the Middle
Ages could cuss all around him. *We* don't know nothing about cussing now-a-days."

"Well," I says, "you needn't cry about it, I reckon we can git along.
Can a bishop cuss, now, the way they useter?"

"Yes, they learn it, because it's part of the polite learning that be-
longs to his lay-out—kind of bells letters, as you may say—and
although he ain't got no more use for it than Missouri girls has for
French, he's got to learn it, same as they do, because a Missouri girl
that can't polly-voo and a bishop that can't cuss ain't got no business
in society."

"Don't they ever cuss at all, now, Tom?"

"Not but very seldom. Praps they do in Peru, but amongst people
that knows anything, it's played out, and they don't mind it no more
than they do Ben Miller's kind. It's because they've got so far along
that they know as much now as the grasshoppers did in the Middle
Ages."

"The grasshoppers?"

"Yes. In the Middle Ages, in France, when the grasshoppers started
in to eat up the crops, the bishop would go out in the fields and pull
a solemn face and give them a most solid good cussing. Just the way
they done with a Jew or a heretic or a king, as I was telling you."

"And what did the grasshoppers do, Tom?"

"Just laughed, and went on and et up the crop, same as they started
in to do. The difference betwixt a man and a grasshopper, in the
Middle Ages, was that the grasshopper warn't a fool."

"Oh, my goodness, oh, my goodness gracious, dah's de lake agin!"
yelled Jim, just then. "*Now*, Mars Tom, what you gwyne to say?"

Yes, sir, there was the lake again, away yonder across the Desert,
perfectly plain, trees and all, just the same as it was before. I says—

"I reckon you're satisfied now, Tom Sawyer."

But he says, perfectly cam—

"Yes, satisfied there ain't no lake there."

Jim says—

"*Don't* talk so, Mars Tom—it sk'yers me to hear you. It's so hot,
en you's so thirsty, dat you ain't in yo' right mine, Mars Tom. Oh,

but don't she look good! 'clah I doan' know how I's gwyne to wait tell
we gits dah, I's *so* thirsty."

"Well, you'll have to wait; and it won't do you no good, either,
because there ain't no lake there, I tell you."

I says—

"Jim, don't you take your eye off of it, and I won't, either."

"'Deed I won't; en bless you, honey, I couldn't ef I wanted to."

We went a-tearing along towards it, piling the miles behind us like
nothing, but never gaining an inch on it—and all of a sudden it was
gone again! Jim staggered, and most fell down. When he got his breath
he says, gasping like a fish—

"Mars Tom, hit's a *ghos'*, dat's what it is, en I hopes to goodness we
ain't gwyne to see it no mo'. Dey's *ben* a lake, en suthin's happened,
en de lake's dead, en we's seen its ghos'; we's seen it twyste, and dat's
proof. De Desert's ha'nted, it's ha'nted, sho'; oh, Mars Tom, le's git
outen it, I druther die than have de night ketch us in it agin en de
ghos' er dat lake come a-mournin' aroun' us en we asleep en doan'
know de danger we's in."

"Ghost, you gander! it ain't anything but air and heat and thirsti-
ness pasted together by a person's imagination. If I—gimme the glass!"

He grabbed it and begun to gaze, off to the right.

"It's a flock of birds," he says. "It's getting towards sundown, and
they're making a bee line across our track for somewheres. They
mean business—maybe they're going for food or water, or both. Let
her go to starboard!—port your hellum! Hard down! There—ease
up—steady, as you go."

We shut down some of the power, so as not to out-speed them,
and took out after them. We went skimming along a quarter of a mile
behind them, and when we had followed them an hour and a half and
was getting pretty discouraged, and thirsty clean to unendurableness,
Tom says—

"Take the glass, one of you, and see what that is, away ahead of
the birds."

Jim got the first glimpse, and slumped down on a locker, sick. He
was most crying, and says—

"She's dah agin, Mars Tom, she's dah agin, en I knows I's gwyne to
die, 'caze when a body sees a ghos' de third time, dat's what it means.
I wisht I'd never come in dis balloon, dat I does."

He wouldn't look no more, and what he said made me afraid, too, because I knowed it was true, for that has always been the way with ghosts; so then I wouldn't look any more, either. Both of us begged Tom to turn off and go some other way, but he wouldn't, and said we was ignorant superstitious blatherskites. Yes, and he'll git come up with, one of these days, I says to myself, insulting ghosts that way. They'll stand it for a while, maybe, but they won't stand it always, for anybody that knows about ghosts knows how easy they are hurt, and how revengeful they are.

So we was all quiet and still, Jim and me being scared, and Tom busy. By and by Tom fetched the balloon to a standstill, and says—

"*Now* get up and look, you sapheads."

We done it, and there was the sure-enough water right under us!— clear, and blue, and cool, and deep, and wavy with the breeze, the loveliest sight that ever was. And all about it was grassy banks, and flowers, and shady groves of big trees, looped together with vines, and all looking so peaceful and comfortable, enough to make a body cry, it was so beautiful.

Jim *did* cry, and rip and dance and carry on, he was so thankful and out of his mind for joy. It was my watch, so I had to stay by the works, but Tom and Jim clumb down and drunk a barrel apiece, and fetched me up a lot, and I've tasted a many a good thing in my life, but nothing that ever begun with that water. Then they went down and had a swim, and then Tom come up and spelled me, and me and Jim had a swim, and then Jim spelled Tom, and me and Tom had a foot-race and a boxing-mill, and I don't reckon I ever had such a good time in my life. It warn't so very hot, because it was close on to evening, and we hadn't any clothes on, anyway. Clothes is well enough in school, and in towns, and at balls, too, but there ain't no sense in them when there ain't no civilization nor other kinds of bothers and fussiness around.

"Lions a-comin'!—lions! Quick, Mars Tom, jump for yo' life, Huck!"

Oh, and didn't we! We never stopped for clothes, but waltzed up the ladder just so. Jim lost his head, straight off—he always done it whenever he got excited and scared; and so now, 'stead of just easing the ladder up from the ground a little, so the animals couldn't reach it, he turned on a raft of power, and we went whizzing up and was dangling in the sky before he got his wits together and seen what a foolish thing he was doing. Then he stopped her, but had clean forgot what to do next; so there we was, so high that the lions looked like pups, and we was drifting off on the wind.

But Tom he shinned up and went for the works and begun to slant her down, and back towards the lake, where the animals was gathering like a camp meeting, and I judged he had lost *his* head, too; for he knowed I was too scared to climb, and did he want to dump me amongst the tigers and things?

But no, his head was level, he knowed what he was about. He swooped down to within thirty or forty foot of the lake, and stopped right over the centre, and sung out—

"Leggo, and drop!"

I done it, and shot down, feet first, and seemed to go about a mile towards the bottom; and when I come up, he says—

"Now lay on your back and float till you're rested and got your pluck back, then I'll dip the ladder in the water and you can climb aboard."

I done it.

Now that was ever so smart in Tom, because if he had started off somewheres else to drop down on the sand, the menagerie would a come along, too, and might a kept us hunting a safe place till I got tuckered out and fell.

And all this time the lions and tigers was sorting out the clothes, and trying to divide them up so there would be some for all, but there was a misunderstanding about it somewheres, on accounts of some of them trying to hog more than their share; so there was another insurrection, and you never see anything like it in the world. There must a been fifty of them, all mixed up together, snorting and roaring and snapping and biting and tearing, legs and tails in the air and you couldn't tell which belonged to which, and the sand and fur a-flying. And when they got done, some was dead, and some was limping off crippled, and the rest was setting around on the battle field, some of them licking their sore places and the others looking up at us and seemed to be kind of inviting us to come down and have some fun, but which we didn't want any.

As for the clothes, there warn't any, any more. Every last rag of them was inside of the animals; and not agreeing with them very

well, I don't reckon, for there was considerable many brass buttons
on them, and there was knives in the pockets, too, and smoking
tobacco, and nails and chalk and marbles and fishhooks and things.
But I wasn't caring. All that was bothering me was, that all we had,
now, was the Professor's clothes, a big enough assortment, but not
suitable to go into company with, if we come across any, because the
britches was as long as tunnels, and the coats and things according.
Still, there was everything a tailor needed, and Jim was a kind of a
jack-legged tailor, and he allowed he could soon trim a suit or two
down for us that would answer.

"AND ALL THIS TIME THE LIONS AND TIGERS WAS SORTING OUT THE CLOTHES."

CHAPTER 9

STILL, WE THOUGHT we would drop down there a minute, but on another errand. Most of the Professor's cargo of food was put up in cans, in the new way that somebody had just invented, the rest was fresh. When you fetch Missouri beefsteak to the Great Sahara, you want to be particular and stay up in the coolish weather. Ours was all right till we stayed down so long amongst the dead people. That spoilt the water, and it ripened up the beefsteak to a degree that was just right for an Englishman, Tom said, but was most too gay for Americans; so we reckoned we would drop down into the lion market and see how we could make out there.

We hauled in the ladder and dropped down till we was just above the reach of the animals, then we let down a rope with a slip-knot in it and hauled up a dead lion, a small tender one, then yanked up a cub tiger. We had to keep the congregation off with the revolver, or they would a took a hand in the proceedings and helped.

We carved off a supply from both, and saved the skins, and hove the rest overboard. Then we baited some of the Professor's hooks with the fresh meat and went a-fishing. We stood over the lake just a convenient distance above the water, and catched a lot of the nicest fish you ever see. It was a most amazing good supper we had: lion steak, tiger steak, fried fish and hot corn pone. I don't want nothing better than that.

We had some fruit to finish off with. We got it out of the top of a monstrous tall tree. It was a very slim tree that hadn't a branch on it from the bottom plum to the top, and there it busted out like a feather-duster. It was a pam tree, of course; anybody knows a pam tree the minute he sees it, by the pictures. We went for coconuts in this one, but there warn't none. There was only big loose bunches of things like over-sized grapes, and Tom allowed they was dates, because he said they answered the description in the Arabian Nights and the other books. Of course they mightn't be, and they might be pison; so we had to wait a spell, and watch and see if the birds et them. They done it; so we done it too, and they was most amazing good.

By this time monstrous big birds begun to come and settle on the dead animals. They was plucky creturs; they would tackle one end of a lion that was being gnawed at the other end by another lion. If the lion drove the bird away, it didn't do no good, he was back again the minute the lion was busy.

The big birds come out of every part of the sky—you could make them out with the glass whilst they was still so far away you couldn't see them with your naked eye. The dead meat was too fresh to have any smell—at least any that could reach to a bird that was five mile away; so Tom said the birds didn't find out the meat was there by the smell, they had to find it out by seeing it. Oh, but ain't that an eye for you! Tom said at the distance of five mile a patch of dead lions couldn't look any bigger than a person's finger nail, and he couldn't imagine how the birds could notice such a little thing so far off.

It was strange and unnatural to see lion eat lion, and we thought maybe they warn't kin. But Jim said that didn't make no difference. He said a hog was fond of her own children, and so was a spider, and he reckoned maybe a lion was pretty near as unprincipled though maybe not quite. He thought likely a lion wouldn't eat his own father, if he knowed which was him, but reckoned he would eat his brother-in-law if he was uncommon hungry, and eat his mother-in-law any time. But *reckoning* don't settle nothing. You can reckon till the cows comes home, but that don't fetch you no decision. So we give it up and let it drop.

Generly it was very still in the Desert, nights, but this time there was music. A lot of other animals come to dinner: sneaking yelpers that Tom allowed was jackals, and roach-backed ones that he said was hyenas; and all the whole biling of them kept up a racket all the time. They made a picture in the moonlight that was more different than any picture I ever see. We had a line out and made fast to the top of a tree, and didn't stand no watch, but all turned in and slept, but I was up two or three times to look down at the animals and hear the music. It was like having a front seat at a menagerie for nothing, which I hadn't ever had before, and so it seemed foolish to sleep and not make the most of it, I mightn't ever have such a chance again.

We went a-fishing again in the early dawn, and then lazied around all day in the deep shade on an island, taking turn about to watch and see that none of the animals come a-snooping around there after erronorts for dinner. We was going to leave next day, but couldn't, it was too lovely.

The day after, when we rose up towards the sky and sailed off eastward, we looked back and watched that place till it warn't nothing but just a speck in the Desert, and I tell you it was like saying good bye to a friend that you ain't ever going to see any more.

Jim was thinking to himself, and at last he says—

"Mars Tom, we's mos' to de end er de Desert now, I speck."

"Why?"

"Well, hit stan' to reason we is. You knows how long we's ben a-skimmin' over it. Mus' be mos' out o' san'. Hit's a wonder to me dat it's hilt out as long as it has."

"Shucks, there's plenty sand, you needn't worry."

"Oh, I ain't a-worryin', Mars Tom, only wonderin', dat's all. De Lord's got plenty san', I ain't doubtin' dat, but nemmine, He ain' gwyne to was'e it jist on dat account; en I allows dat dis Desert's plenty big enough now, jist de way she is, en you can't spread her out no mo' 'dout was'in' san'."

"Oh, go 'long! we ain't much more than fairly *started* across this Desert yet. The United States is a pretty big country, ain't it? Ain't it, Huck?"

"Yes," I says, "there ain't no bigger one, I don't reckon."

"Well," he says, "this Desert is about the shape of the United States, and if you was to lay it down on top of the United States, it would cover the land of the free out of sight like a blanket. There'd be a little corner sticking out, up at Maine and away up north-west, and Florida sticking out like a turtle's tail, and that's all. We've took California away from the Mexicans two or three years ago, so that part of the Pacific coast is ours, now, and if you laid the Great Sahara down with her edge on the Pacific she would cover the United States and stick out past New York six hundred miles into the Atlantic ocean."

I says—

"Good land! have you got the documents for that, Tom Sawyer?"

"Yes, and they're right here, and I've been studying them. You can look for yourself. From New York to the Pacific is 2,600 miles. From one end of the Great Desert to the other is 3,200. The United States contains 3,600,000 square miles, the Desert contains 4,162,000. With the Desert's bulk you could cover up every last inch of the United States, and in under where the edges projected out, you could tuck England, Scotland, Ireland, France, Denmark, and all Germany. Yes, sir, you could hide the home of the brave and all of them countries clean out of sight under the Great Sahara, and you would still have 2,000 square miles of sand left."

"Well," I says, "it clean beats me. Why, Tom, it shows that the Lord took as much pains making this Desert as He did to make the United States and all them other countries. I reckon He must a been a-working at this Desert two or three days before He got it done."

Jim says—

"Huck, dat doan' stan' to reason. I reckon dis Desert wan't made, at all. Now you take en look at it like dis—you look at it, and see ef I's right. What's a desert good for? 'Tain't good for nuthin'. Dey ain't no way to make it pay. Hain't dat so, Huck?"

"Yes, I reckon."

"Hain't it so, Mars Tom?"

"I guess so. Go on."

"Ef a thing ain't no good, it's made in vain, ain't it?"

"Yes."

"*Now*, den! Do de Lord make anything in vain? You answer me dat."

"Well—no, He don't."

"Den how come He make a desert?"

"Well, go on. How *did* He come to make it?"

"Mars Tom, it's my opinion He never *made* it, at all; dat is, He didn't plan out no desert, never sot out to make one. Now I's gwyne to show you, den you kin see. *I* b'lieve it uz jes' like when you's buildin' a house; dey's allays a lot o' truck en rubbish lef' over. What does you do wid it? Doan' you take en k'yart it off en dump it onto a ole vacant back lot? 'Course. Now, den, it's my opinion hit was jes' like dat. When de Lord uz gwyne to buil' de worl', He tuck en made a lot o' rocks en put 'em in a pile, en made a lot o' yearth en put it in a pile handy to de rocks, den a lot o' san', en put dat in a pile, handy, too. Den He begin. He measure out some rocks en yearth en san', en stick 'em together en say 'Dat's Germany,' en pas'e a label on it en set it out to dry; en measure out some mo' rocks en yearth en san', en stick 'em together, en say, 'Dat's de United States,' en pas'e a label on it and set *it* out to dry—en so on, en so on, tell it come supper time Sataday, en He look roun' en see dey's all done, en a mighty good worl' for de time she took. Den He notice dat whilst He's cal'lated de yearth en de rocks jes' right, dey's a mos' turrible lot o' san' lef' over, which He can't 'member how it happened. So He look roun' to see if dey's any ole back lot anywheres dat's vacant, en see dis place, en is pow'ful glad, en tell de angels to take en dump de san' here. Now, den, dat's *my* idea 'bout it—dat de Great Sahara warn't *made* at all, she jes' *happen'*."

I said it was a real good argument, and I believed it was the best one Jim ever made. Tom he said the same, but said the trouble about arguments is, they ain't nothing but *theories*, after all, and theories don't prove nothing, they only give you a place to rest on, a spell, when you are tuckered out butting around and around trying to find out something there ain't no way *to* find out. And he says—

"There's another trouble about theories: there's always a hole in them somewheres, sure, if you look close enough. It's just so with this one of Jim's. Look what billions and billions of stars there is. How does it come that there was just exactly enough star-stuff, and none left over? How does it come there ain't no sand-pile up there?"

But Jim was fixed for him and says—

"What's de Milky Way?—dat's what *I* wants to know. What's de Milky Way? Answer me dat!"

In my opinion it was just a sockdologer. It's only an opinion, it's only *my* opinion, and others may think different; but I said it then and I stand to it now—it was a sockdologer. And moreover besides, it landed Tom Sawyer. He couldn't say a word. He had that stunned look of a person that's been shot in the back with a kag of nails. All he said was, as for people like me and Jim, he'd just as soon have intellectual intercourse with a catfish. But anybody can say that—and I notice they always do, when somebody has fetched them a lifter. Tom Sawyer was tired of that end of the subject.

So we got back to talking about the size of the Desert again, and the more we compared it with this and that and t'other thing, the more nobler and bigger and grander it got to look, right along. And so, hunting amongst the figgers, Tom found, by and by, that it was just the

same size as the Empire of China. Then he showed us the spread the
Empire of China made on the map and the room she took up in the
world. Well, it was wonderful to think of, and I says—

"Why, I've heard talk about this Desert plenty of times, but *I* never
knowed, before, how important she was."

Then Tom says—

"Important! Sahara important! That's just the way with some
people. If a thing's big, it's important. That's all the sense they've got.
All they can see is *size*. Why, look at England. It's the most important
country in the world; and yet you could put it in China's vest pocket;
and not only that, but you'd have the dickens's own time to find it
again the next time you wanted it. And look at Russia. It spreads all
around and everywheres, and yet ain't no more important in this
world than Rhode Island is, and hasn't got half as much in it that's
worth saving. My Uncle Abner, which was a Presbyterian preacher
and the bluest they made, *he* always said that if *size* was a right thing
to judge importance by, where would heaven be, alongside of the other
place? He always said heaven was the Rhode Island of the Hereafter."

Away off, now, we see a low hill, a-standing up just on the edge of
the world. Tom broke off his talk, and reached for a glass very much
excited, and took a look, and says—

"That's it—it's the one I've been looking for, sure. If I'm right, it's
the one the dervish took the man into and showed him all the treasures of the world."

So we begun to gaze, and he begun to tell about it out of the Arabian
Nights.

CHAPTER 10

TOM SAID it happened like this.

A dervish was stumping it along through the Desert, on foot, one blazing hot day, and he had come a thousand miles and was pretty poor, and hungry, and ornery and tired, and along about where we are now, he run across a camel driver with a hundred camels, and asked him for some ams. But the camel driver he asked to be excused. The dervish says—

"Don't you own these camels?"

"Yes, they're mine."

"Are you in debt?"

"Who—me? No."

"Well, a man that owns a hundred camels and ain't in debt, is rich—and not only rich, but very rich. Ain't it so?"

The camel driver owned up that it was so. Then the dervish says—

"God has made you rich, and He has made me poor. He has His reasons, and they are wise, blessed be his Name! But He has willed that His rich shall help His poor, and you have turned away from me, your brother, in my need, and He will remember this, and you will lose by it."

That made the camel driver feel shaky, but all the same he was born hoggish after money and didn't like to let go a cent, so he begun to whine and explain, and said times was hard, and although he had took a full freight down to Balsora and got a fat rate for it, he couldn't git no return freight, and so he warn't making no great things out of his trip. So the dervish starts along again, and says—

"All right, if you want to take the risk, but I reckon you've made a mistake this time, and missed a chance."

Of course the camel driver wanted to know what kind of a chance he had missed, because maybe there was money in it; so he run after the dervish and begged him so hard and earnest to take pity on him and tell him, that at last the dervish give in, and says—

"Do you see that hill yonder? Well, in that hill is all the treasures of the earth, and I was looking around for a man with a particular good kind heart and a noble generous disposition, because if I could find just that man, I've got a kind of a salve I could put on his eyes and he could see the treasures and get them out."

So then the camel driver was in a sweat; and he cried, and begged, and took on, and went down on his knees, and said he was just that kind of a man, and said he could fetch a thousand people that would say he wasn't ever described so exact before.

"Well, then," says the dervish, "all right. If we load the hundred camels, can I have half of them?"

The driver was so glad he couldn't hardly hold in, and says—

"Now you're shouting."

So they shook hands on the bargain, and the dervish got out his box and rubbed the salve on the driver's right eye, and the hill opened and he went in, and there, sure enough, was piles and piles of gold and jewels sparkling like all the stars in heaven had fell down.

So him and the dervish laid into it and they loaded every camel till he couldn't carry no more, then they said good bye, and each of them started off with his fifty. But pretty soon the camel driver come a-running and overtook the dervish and says—

"You ain't in society, you know, and you don't really need all you've got. Won't you be good, and let me have ten of your camels?"

"Well," the dervish says, "I don't know but what you say is reasonable enough."

So he done it, and they separated and the dervish started off again with his forty. But pretty soon here comes the camel driver bawling after him again, and whines and slobbers around and begs another ten off of him, saying thirty camel loads of treasures was enough to see a dervish through, because they live very simple, you know, and don't keep house but board around and give their note.

But that warn't the end, yet. That ornery hound kept coming and coming till he had begged back all the camels and had the whole hundred. Then he was satisfied, and ever so grateful, and said he wouldn't ever forget the dervish as long as he lived, and nobody hadn't ever been so good to him before, and liberal. So they shook hands good bye, and separated and started off again.

But do you know, it warn't ten minutes till the camel driver was

THE CAMEL DRIVER IN THE TREASURE-CAVE.

unsatisfied again—he was the low-downest reptyle in seven counties
—and he come a-running again. And this time the thing he wanted
was to get the dervish to rub some of the salve on his other eye.

"Why?" says the dervish.

"Oh, you know," says the driver.

"Know what?" says the dervish.

"Well, you can't fool me," says the driver. "You're trying to keep back something from me, you know it mighty well. You know, I reckon, that if I had the salve on the other eye I could see a lot more things that's valuable. Come—please put it on."

The dervish says—

"I wasn't keeping anything back from you. I don't mind telling you what would happen if I put it on. You'd never see again. You'd be stone blind the rest of your days."

But do you know, that beat wouldn't believe him. No, he begged and begged, and whined and cried, till at last the dervish opened his box and told him to put it on, if he wanted to. So the man done it, and sure enough he was as blind as a bat, in a minute.

Then the dervish laughed at him and mocked at him and made fun of him, and says—

"Good-bye—a man that's blind hain't got no use for jewelry."

And he cleared out with the hundred camels, and left that man to wander around poor and miserable and friendless the rest of his days in the desert.

Jim said he'd bet it was a lesson to him.

"Yes," Tom says, "and like a considerable many lessons a body gets. They ain't no account, because the thing don't ever happen the same way again—and can't. The time Hen Scovil fell down the chimbly and crippled his back for life, everybody said it would be a lesson to him. What kind of a lesson? How was he going to use it? He couldn't climb chimblies no more, and he hadn't no more backs to break."

"All de same, Mars Tom, dey *is* sich a thing as learnin' by expe'ence. De Good Book say de burnt chile shun de fire."

"Well, I ain't denying that a thing's a lesson if it's a thing that can happen twice just the same way. There's lots of such things, and *they* educate a person, that's what uncle Abner always said; but there's forty *million* lots of the other kind—the kind that don't happen the same way twice—and they ain't no real use, they ain't no more instructive than the small pox. When you've got it, it ain't no good to find out you ought to been vaccinated, and it ain't no good to get vaccinated afterwards, because the small-pox don't come but once. But on the other hand Uncle Abner said that the person that had took a bull by the tail once had learnt sixty or seventy times as much as a person that hadn't; and said a person that started in to carry a cat home by the tail was gitting knowledge that was always going to be useful to him, and warn't ever going to grow dim or doubtful. But I can tell you, Jim, Uncle Abner was down on them people that's all the time trying to dig a lesson out of everything that happens, no matter whether—"

But Jim was asleep. Tom looked kind of ashamed, because you know a person always feels bad when he is talking uncommon fine, and thinks the other person is admiring, and that other person goes to sleep that way. Of course he oughtn't to go to sleep, because it's shabby, but the finer a person talks the certainer it is to make you sleepy, and so when you come to look at it it ain't nobody's fault in particular, both of them's to blame.

Jim begun to snore—soft and blubbery, at first, then a long rasp, then a stronger one, then a half a dozen horrible ones like the last water sucking down the plug-hole of a bath-tub, then the same with more power to it, and some big coughs and snorts flung in, the way a cow does that is choking to death; and when the person has got to that point he is at his level best, and can wake up a man that is in the next block with a dipper-full of loddanum in him, but can't wake himself up, although all that awful noise of his'n ain't but three inches from his own ears. And that is the curiosest thing in the world, seems to me. But you rake a match to light the candle, and that little bit of a noise will fetch him. I wish I knowed what was the reason of that, but there don't seem to be no way to find out. Now there was Jim alarming the whole Desert, and yanking the animals out, for miles and miles around, to see what in the nation was going on up there; there warn't nobody nor nothing that was as close to the noise as *he* was, and yet he was the only cretur that wasn't disturbed by it. We yelled at him and whooped at him, it never done no good, but the first time there come a little wee noise that wasn't of a usual kind it woke him up. No, sir, I've thought it all over, and so has Tom, and there ain't no way to find out why a snorer can't hear himself snore.

Jim said he hadn't been asleep, he just shut his eyes so he could listen better.

Tom said nobody warn't accusing him.

That made him look like he wished he hadn't said anything. And he wanted to git away from the subject, I reckon, because he begun to

abuse the camel driver, just the way a person does when he has got
catched in something and wants to take it out of somebody else. He let
into the camel driver the hardest he knowed how, and I had to agree
with him; and he praised up the dervish the highest he could, and I
had to agree with him there, too. But Tom says—

"I ain't so sure. You call that dervish so dreadful liberal and good and
unselfish, but I don't quite see it. He didn't hunt up another poor
dervish, did he? No, he didn't. If he was so unselfish, why didn't he go
in there himself and take a pocket full of jewels and go along and be
satisfied? No, sir, the person he was hunting for was a man with a
hundred camels. He wanted to get away with all the treasure he
could."

"Why, Mars Tom, he was willin' to divide, fair and square; he
only struck for fifty camels."

"Because he knowed how he was going to get all of them by and by."

"Mars Tom, he *tole* de man de truck would make him bline."

"Yes, because he knowed the man's character. It was just the kind of
a man he was hunting for—a man that never believes in anybody's
word or anybody's honorableness, because he ain't got none of his
own. I reckon there's lots of people like that dervish. They swindle,
right and left, but they always make the other person *seem* to swindle
himself. They keep inside of the letter of the law all the time, and there
ain't no way to git hold of them. *They* don't put the salve on—oh, no,
that would be sin; but they know how to fool *you* into putting it on,
then it's you that blinds yourself. I reckon the dervish and the camel
driver was just a pair—a fine, smart, brainy rascal, and a dull, coarse,
ignorant one, but both of them rascals, just the same."

"Mars Tom, does you reckon dey's any o' dat kind o' salve in de
worl' now?"

"Yes, uncle Abner says there is. He says they've got it in New York,
and they put it on country people's eyes and show them all the
railroads in the world, and they go in and git them, and then when
they rub the salve on the other eye, the other man bids them good bye
and goes off with their railroads. Here's the treasure-hill, now. Lower
away!"

We landed, but it warn't as interesting as I thought it was going to be,
because we couldn't find the place where they went in to git the
treasure. Still, it was plenty interesting enough, just to see the mere hill

itself where such a wonderful thing happened. Jim said he wouldn't a missed it for three dollars, and I felt the same way.

And to me and Jim, as wonderful a thing as any, was the way Tom could come into a strange big country like this and go straight and find a little hump like that and tell it in a minute from a million other humps that was almost just like it, and nothing to help him but only his own learning and his own natural smartness. We talked and talked it over together, but couldn't make out how he done it. He had the best head on him I ever see; and all he lacked was age, to make a name for himself equal to Captain Kidd or George Washington. I bet you it would a crowded either of *them* to find that hill, with all their gifts, but it warn't nothing to Tom Sawyer; he went across Sahara and put his finger on it as easy as you could pick a nigger out of a bunch of angels.

We found a pond of salt water close by and scraped up a raft of salt around the edges and loaded up the lion's skin and the tiger's so as they would keep till Jim could tan them.

CHAPTER 11

W̲E̲ ̲W̲E̲N̲T̲ ̲A̲-̲F̲O̲O̲L̲I̲N̲G̲ along for a day or two, and then just as the full moon was touching the ground on the other side of the Desert, we see a string of little black figgers moving across its big silver face. You could see them as plain as if they was painted on the moon with ink. It was another caravan. We cooled down our speed and tagged along after it just to have company, though it warn't going our way. It was a rattler, that caravan, and a most bully sight to look at, next morning when the sun come a-streaming across the Desert and flung the long shadders of the camels on the gold sand like a thousand grand-daddy-longlegses marching in procession. We never went very near it, because we knowed better, now, than to act like that and scare people's camels and break up their caravans. It was the gayest outfit you ever see, for rich clothes and nobby style. Some of the chiefs rode on dromedaries, the first we ever see, and very tall, and they go plunging along like they was on stilts, and they rock the man that is on them pretty violent and churn up his dinner considerable, I bet you, but they make noble good time and a camel ain't nowheres with them for speed.

The caravan camped, during the middle part of the day, and then started again about the middle of the afternoon. Before long the sun begun to look very curious. First it kind of turned to brass, and then to copper, and after that it begun to look like a blood red ball, and the air got hot and close, and pretty soon all the sky in the west darkened up and looked thick and foggy, but fiery and dreadful like it looks through a piece of red glass, you know. We looked down and see a big confusion going on in the caravan and a rushing every which way like they was scared, and then they all flopped down flat in the sand and laid there perfectly still.

Pretty soon we see something coming that stood up like an amazing wide wall, and reached from the Desert up into the sky and hid the sun, and it was coming like the nation, too. Then a little faint breeze struck us, and then it come harder, and grains of sand begun to sift against our faces and sting like fire, and Tom sung out—

"It's a sand-storm—turn your backs to it!"

We done it, and in another minute it was blowing a gale and the sand beat against us by the shovelfull and the air was so thick with it we couldn't see a thing. In five minutes the boat was level full and we was setting on the lockers buried up to the chin in sand and only our heads out and could hardly breathe.

IN THE SAND-STORM.

Then the storm thinned, and we see that monstrous wall go a-sailing off across the Desert, awful to look at, I tell you. We dug ourselves out and looked down, and where the caravan was before, there wasn't anything but just the sand ocean, now and all still and quiet. All them people and camels was smothered and dead and buried—buried under ten foot of sand, we reckoned, and Tom allowed it might be years before the wind uncovered them, and all that time their friends wouldn't ever know what become of that caravan. Tom said—

"Now we know what it was that happened to the people we got the swords and pistols from."

Yes, sir, that was just it. It was as plain as day, now. They got buried in a sand-storm, and the wild animals couldn't get at them, and the wind never uncovered them again till they was dried to leather and warn't fit to eat. It seemed to me we had felt as sorry for them poor people as a person could for anybody, and as mournful, too, but we was mistaken; this last caravan's death went harder with us, a good deal harder. You see, the others was total strangers, and we never got to feeling acquainted with them at all, except, maybe, a little with the man that was watching the girl, but it was different with this last caravan. We was huvvering around them a whole night and most a whole day, and had got to feeling real friendly with them, and acquainted. I have found out that there ain't no surer way to find out whether you like people or hate them, than to travel with them. Just so with these. We kind of liked them from the start, and traveling with them put on the finisher. The longer we traveled with them, and the more we got used to their ways, the better and better we liked them and the gladder and gladder we was that we run across them. We had come to know some of them so well that we called them by name when we was talking about them, and soon got so familiar and sociable that we even dropped the Miss and the Mister and just used their plain names without any handle, and it did not seem unpolite, but just the right thing. Of course it wasn't their own names, but names we give them. There was Mr. Elexander Robinson and Miss Adaline Robinson, and Col. Jacob McDougal and Miss Harryet McDougal, and Judge Jeremiah Butler and young Bushrod Butler, and these was big chiefs, mostly, that wore splendid great turbans and simmeters, and dressed like the Grand Mogul, and their families. But as soon as we come to know them good, and like them very much, it warn't Mister, nor

Judge, nor nothing, any more, but only Elleck, and Addy, and Jake, and Hattie, and Jerry and Buck, and so on.

And you know, the more you join in with people in their joys and their sorrows, the more nearer and dearer they come to be to you. Now we warn't cold and indifferent, the way most travelers is, we was right down friendly and sociable, and took a chance in everything that was

THE WEDDING PROCESSION.

going, and the caravan could depend on us to be on hand every time, it didn't make no difference what it was.

When they camped, we camped right over them, ten or twelve hundred foot up in the air. When they et a meal, we et ourn, and it made it ever so much homeliker to have their company. When they had a wedding, that night, and Buck and Addy got married, we got ourselves up in the very starchiest of the Professor's duds for the blow-out, and when they danced we joined in and shook a foot up there.

But it is sorrow and trouble that brings you the nearest, and it was a

funeral that done it with us. It was next morning, just in the still dawn.
We didn't know the diseased, and he warn't in our set, but that never
made no difference, he belonged to the caravan, and that was enough,
and there warn't no more sincerer tears shed over him than the ones
we dripped on him from up there eleven hundred foot on high.

"WHEN THEY DANCED WE JOINED IN AND SHOOK A FOOT UP THERE."

Yes, parting with this caravan was much more bitterer than it was to part with them others, which was comparative strangers, and been dead so long, anyway. We had knowed these in their lives, and was fond of them, too, and now to have death snatch them from right before our faces whilst we was looking, and leave us so lonesome and friendless in the middle of that big Desert, it did hurt so, and we wished we mightn't ever make any more friends on that voyage if we was going to lose them again like that.

We couldn't keep from talking about them, and they was all the time coming up in our memory, and looking just the way they looked when we was all alive and happy together. We could see the line marching, and the shiny spear-heads a-winking in the sun, we could see the dromedaries lumbering along, we could see the wedding and the funeral, and more oftener than anything else we could see them praying, because they didn't allow nothing to prevent that; whenever the call come, several times a day, they would stop right there, and stand up and face to the east, and lift back their heads, and spread out their arms and begin, and four or five times they would go down on their knees, and then fall forwards and touch their forehead to the ground.

Well, it warn't good to go on talking about them, lovely as they was in their life, and dear to us in their life and death both, because it didn't do no good, and made us too down-hearted. Jim allowed he was going to live as good a life as he could, so he could see them again in a better world; and Tom kept still and didn't tell him they was only Mahometans, it warn't no use to disappoint him, he was feeling bad enough just as it was.

When we woke up next morning we was feeling a little cheerfuller, and had had a most powerful good sleep, because sand is the comfortablest bed there is, and I don't see why people that can afford it don't have it more. And it's terrible good ballast, too; I never see the balloon so steady before.

Tom allowed we had twenty tons of it, and wondered what we better do with it; it was good sand, and it didn't seem good sense to throw it away. Jim says—

"Mars Tom, can't we tote it back home en sell it? How long 'll it take?"

"Depends on the way we go."

"Well, sah, she's wuth a quarter of a dollar a load, at home, en I reckon we's got as much as twenty loads, hain't we? How much would dat be?"

"Five dollars."

"By jings, Mars Tom, le's shove for home right on de spot! Hit's more'n a dollar en a half apiece, hain't it?"

"Yes."

"Well, ef dat ain't makin' money de easiest ever *I* struck! She jes' rained in—never cos' us a lick o' work. Le's mosey right along, Mars Tom."

But Tom was thinking and ciphering away so busy and excited he never heard him. Pretty soon he says—

"Five dollars—sho! Look here, this sand's worth—worth—why, it's worth no end of money."

"How is dat, Mars Tom? Go on, honey, go on!"

"Well, the minute people knows it's genuwyne sand from the genuwyne Desert of Sahara, they'll just be in a perfect state of mind to git hold of some of it to keep on the what-not in a vial with a label on it for a curiosity. All we got to do, is, to put it up in vials and float around all over the United States and peddle them out at ten cents apiece. We've got all of ten thousand dollars' worth of sand in this boat."

Me and Jim went all to pieces with joy, and begun to shout whoopjamboreehoo, and Tom says—

"And we can keep on coming back and fetching sand, and coming back and fetching more sand, and just keep it a-going till we've carted this whole Desert over there and sold it out; and there ain't ever going to be any opposition, either, because we'll take out a patent."

"My goodness," I says, "we'll be as rich as Creeosote, won't we, Tom?"

"Yes—Creesus, you mean. Why, that dervish was hunting in that little hill for the treasures of the earth, and didn't know he was walking over the real ones for a thousand miles. He was blinder than he made the driver."

"Mars Tom, how much is we gwyne to be wuth?"

"Well, I don't know, yet. It's got to be ciphered, and it ain't the easiest job to do, either, because it's over four million square miles of sand at ten cents a vial."

Jim was awful excited, but this faded it out considerable, and he shook his head and says—

"Mars Tom, we can't 'ford all dem vials—a king couldn't. We better not try to take de whole Desert, Mars Tom, de vials gwyne to bust us, sho'."

Tom's excitement died out, too, now, and I reckoned it was on account of the vials, but it wasn't. He set there thinking, and got bluer and bluer, and at last he says—

"Boys, it won't work; we got to give it up."

"Why, Tom?"

"On account of the duties."

I couldn't make nothing out of that, neither could Jim. I says—

"What *is* our duty, Tom? Because if we can't git around it, why can't we just *do* it? People often has to."

But he says—

"Oh, it ain't that kind of duty. The kind I mean is a tax. Whenever you strike a frontier—that's the border of a country, you know—you find a custom house there, and the gov'ment officers comes and rummages amongst your things and charges a big tax, which they call a duty because it's their duty to bust you if they can, and if you don't pay the duty they'll hog your sand. They call it confiscating, but that don't deceive nobody, it's just hogging, and that's all it is. Now if we try to carry this sand home the way we're pointed now, we got to climb fences till we git tired—just frontier after frontier—Egypt, Arabia, Hindostan, and so on, and they'll all whack on a duty, and so you see, easy enough, we *can't go that* road."

"Why, Tom," I says, "we can sail right over their old frontiers; how are *they* going to stop us?"

He looked sorrowful at me, and says, very grave—

"Huck Finn, do you think that would be honest?"

I hate them kind of interruptions. I never said nothing, and he went on—

"Well, we're shut off the other way, too. If we go back the way we've come, there's the New York custom house, and that is worse than all of them others put together, on account of the kind of cargo we've got."

"Why?"

"Well, they can't raise Sahara sand in America, of course, and when they can't raise a thing there, the duty is fourteen hundred thousand per cent on it if you try to fetch it in from where they do raise it."

"There ain't no sense in that, Tom Sawyer."

"Who said there *was*? What do you talk to me like that, for, Huck Finn? You wait till I say a thing's got sense in it before you go to accusing me of saying it."

"All right, consider me crying about it, and sorry. Go on."

Jim says—

"Mars Tom, do dey jam dat duty onto everything we can't raise in America, en don't make no 'stinction twix' anything?"

"Yes, that's what they do."

"Mars Tom, ain't de blessin' o' de Lord de mos' valuable thing dey is?"

"Yes, it is."

"Don't de preacher stan' up in de pulpit en call it down on de people?"

"Yes."

"Whah do it come from?"

"From heaven."

"Yassir! You's jes' right, 'deed you is, honey—it come from heaven, en dat's a foreign country. *Now* den! do dey put a tax on dat blessin'?"

"No, they don't."

"'Course dey don't; en so it stan' to reason dat you's mistaken, Mars Tom. Dey wouldn't put de tax on po' truck like san', dat nobody ain't 'bleeged to have, en leave it off'n de bes' thing dey is, which nobody can't git along widout."

Tom Sawyer was stumped; he see Jim had got him where he couldn't budge. He tried to wiggle out by saying they had *forgot* to put on that tax, but they'd be sure to remember about it, next session of Congress, and then they'd put it on, but that was a poor lame come-off, and he knowed it. He said there warn't nothing foreign that warn't taxed but just that one, and so they couldn't be consistent without taxing it, and to be consistent was the first law of politics. So he stuck to it that they'd left it out unintentional and would be certain to do their best to fix it before they got caught and laughed at.

But I didn't feel no more interest in such things, as long as we couldn't git our sand through, and it made me low-spirited, and Jim the same. Tom he tried to cheer us up by saying he would think up another speculation for us that would be just as good as this one and better, but it didn't do no good, we didn't believe there was any as big as this. It was mighty hard; such a little while ago we was so rich, and could a bought a country and started a kingdom and been celebrated and happy, and now we was so poor and ornery again, and had our sand left on our hands. The sand was looking so lovely, before, just like gold and di'monds, and the feel of it was so soft and so silky and nice, but now I couldn't bear the sight of it, it made me sick to look at it, and I knowed I wouldn't ever feel comfortable again till we got shut of it, and didn't have it there no more to remind us of what we had been and what we had got degraded down to. The others was feeling the same way about it that I was. I knowed it, because they cheered up so, the minute I says le's throw this truck overboard.

Well, it was going to be work, you know, and pretty solid work, too; so Tom he divided it up according to fairness and strength. He said me and him would clear out a fifth apiece, of the sand, and Jim three fifths. Jim he didn't quite like that arrangement. He says—

"'Course I's de stronges', en I's willin' to do a share accordin', but by jings you's kinder pilin' it onto ole Jim, Mars Tom, hain't you?"

"Well, I didn't think so, Jim, but you try your hand at fixing it, and let's see."

So Jim he reckoned it wouldn't be no more than fair if me and Tom done a *tenth* apiece. Tom he turned his back to git room and be private, and then he smole a smile that spread around and covered the whole Sahara to the westard, back to the Atlantic edge of it where we come from. Then he turned around again and said it was a good enough arrangement, and we was satisfied if Jim was. Jim said he was.

So then Tom measured off our two tenths in the bow and left the rest for Jim, and it surprised Jim a good deal to see how much difference there was and what a raging lot of sand his share come to, and said he was powerful glad, now, that he had spoke up in time and got the first arrangement altered, for he said that even the way it was now, there was more sand than enjoyment in his end of the contract, he believed.

Then we laid into it. It was mighty hot work, and tough; so hot we had to move up into cooler weather or we couldn't a stood it. Me and Tom took turn about, and one worked while t'other rested, but there warn't nobody to spell poor old Jim, and he made all that part of Africa damp, he sweated so. We couldn't work good, we was so full of laugh, and Jim he kept fretting and wanting to know what tickled us so, and we had to keep making up things to account for it, and they was pretty

CHAPTER 12

THE NEXT FEW MEALS was pretty sandy, but that don't make no difference when you are hungry, and when you ain't it ain't no satisfaction to eat, anyway, and so a little grit in the meat ain't no particular drawback, as far as I can see.

Then we struck the east end of the Desert at last, sailing on a north-east course. Away off on the edge of the sand, in a soft pinky light, we see three little sharp roofs like tents, and Tom says—

"It's the Pyramids of Egypt."

It made my heart fairly jump. You see, I had seen a many and a many a picture of them, and heard tell about them a hundred times, and yet to come on them all of a sudden, that way, and find they was *real*, 'stead of imaginations, most knocked the breath out of me with surprise. It's a curious thing, that the more you hear about a grand and big and bully thing or person, the more it kind of dreamies out, as you may say, and gets to be a big dim wavery figger made out of moonshine and nothing solid to it. It's just so with George Washington, and the same with them Pyramids.

And moreover besides, the things they always said about them seemed to me to be stretchers. There was a feller come to the Sunday school, once, and had a picture of them, and made a speech, and said the biggest Pyramid covered thirteen acres, and was most five hundred foot high, just a steep mountain, all built out of hunks of stone as big as a bureau, and laid up in perfectly regular layers, like stair-steps. Thirteen acres, you see, for just one building; it's a farm. If it hadn't been in Sunday school, I would a judged it was a lie; and outside I was certain of it. And he said there was a hole in the Pyramid, and you could go in there with candles, and go ever so far up a long slanting tunnel, and come to a large room in the stomach of that stone mountain, and there you would find a big stone chest with a king in it, four thousand years old. I said to myself, then, if that ain't a lie I will eat

that king if they will fetch him, for even Methusalem warn't that old,
and nobody claims it.

As we come a little nearer we see the yaller sand come to an end in a
long straight edge like a blanket, and onto it was joined, edge to edge, a
wide country of bright green, with a snaky stripe crooking through it,

and Tom said it was the Nile. It made my heart jump again, for the
Nile was another thing that wasn't real to me. Now I can tell you one
thing which is dead certain: if you will fool along over three thousand
miles of yaller sand, all glimmery with heat so that it makes your eyes
water to look at it, and you've been a considerable part of a week doing
it, the green country will look so like home and heaven to you that it
will make your eyes water *again*. It was just so with me, and the same
with Jim.

And when Jim got so he could believe it *was* the land of Egypt he was
looking at, he wouldn't enter it standing up, but got down on his knees
and took off his hat, because he said it wasn't fitten for a humble poor
nigger to come any other way where such men had been as Moses and
Joseph and Pharaoh and the other prophets. He was a Presbyterian, and
had a most deep respect for Moses, which was a Presbyterian too, he
said. He was all stirred up, and says—

"Hit's de lan' of Egypt, de lan' of Egypt, en I's 'lowed to look at it wid
my own eyes! En dah's de river dat was turn' to blood, en I's lookin' at
de very same groun' whah de plagues was, en de lice, en de frogs, en de
locus', en de hail, en whah dey marked de door-pos', en de angel o' de
Lord come by in de darkness o' de night en slew de fust-born in all de
lan' of Egypt. Ole Jim ain't worthy to see dis day!"

And then he just broke down and cried, he was so thankful. So
between him and Tom there was talk enough, Jim being excited
because the land was so full of history—Joseph and his brethren,
Moses in the bulrushers, Jacob coming down into Egypt to buy corn,
the silver cup in the sack, and all them interesting things, and Tom just

as excited too, because the land was so full of history that was in *his* line, about Noureddin, and Bedreddin, and such like monstrous giants, that made Jim's wool rise, and a raft of other Arabian Nights folks, which the half of them never done the things they let on they done, I don't believe.

Then we struck a disappointment, for one of them early-morning fogs started up, and it warn't no use to sail over the top of it, because we would go by Egypt, sure, so we judged it was best to set her by compass straight for the place where the Pyramids was gitting blurred and blotted out, and then drop low and skin along pretty close to the ground and keep a sharp lookout. Tom took the hellum, I stood by to let go the anchor, and Jim he straddled the bow to dig through the fog with his eyes and watch out for danger ahead. We went along a steady gait, but not very fast, and the fog got solider and solider, so solid that Jim looked dim and ragged and smoky through it. It was awful still, and we talked low and was anxious. Now and then Jim would say—

"Highst her a pint, Mars Tom, highst her!" and up she would skip, a foot or two, and we would slide right over a flat-roofed mud cabin, with people that had been asleep on it just beginning to turn out and gap and stretch; and once when a feller was clear up on his hind legs so he could gap and stretch better, we took him a blip in the back and knocked him off. By and by, after about an hour, and everything dead still and we a-straining our ears for sounds and holding our breath, the fog thinned a little, very sudden, and Jim sung out in an awful scare—

"Oh, for de lan's sake, set her back, Mars Tom, here's de biggest giant outen de 'Rabian Nights a-comin' for us!" and he went over backwards in the boat.

Tom slammed on the back-action, and as we slowed to a stand-still, a man's face as big as our house at home looked in over the gunnel, same as a house looks out of its windows, and I laid down and died. I must a been clear dead and gone for as much as a minute or more; then I come to, and Tom had hitched a boat-hook onto the lower lip of the giant and was holding the balloon steady with it whilst he canted his head back and got a good long look up at that awful face.

Jim was on his knees with his hands clasped, gazing up at the thing in a begging way, and working his lips but not getting anything out. I took only just a glimpse, and was fading out again, but Tom says—

"He ain't alive, you fools, it's the Sphynx!"

I never see Tom look so little and like a fly; but that was because the giant's head was so big and awful. Awful, yes, so it was, but not dreadful, any more, because you could see it was a noble face, and kind of sad, and not thinking about you, but about other things and larger. It was stone, reddish stone, and its nose and ears battered, and that give it an abused look, and you felt sorrier for it for that.

We stood off a piece, and sailed around it and over it, and it was just grand. It was a man's head, or maybe a woman's, on a tiger's body a hundred and twenty-five foot long, and there was a dear little temple between its front paws. All but the head used to be under the sand, for hundreds of years, maybe thousands, but they had just lately dug the sand away and found that little temple. It took a power of sand to bury that cretur; most as much as it would to bury a steamboat, I reckon.

We landed Jim on top of the head, with an American flag to protect him, it being a foreign land, then we sailed off to this and that and t'other distance, to git what Tom called effects and perspectives and proportions, and Jim he done the best he could, striking all the different kinds of attitudes and positions he could study up, but standing on his head and working his legs the way a frog does was the best. The further we got away, the littler Jim got, and the grander the Sphinx got, till at last it was only a clothes-pin on a dome, as you might say. That's the way perspective brings out the correct proportions, Tom said; he said Julus Cesar's niggers didn't know how big he was, they was too close to him.

Then we sailed off further and further, till we couldn't see Jim at all, any more, and then that great figger was at its noblest, a-gazing out over the Nile valley so still and solemn and lonesome, and all the little shabby huts and things that was scattered about it clean disappeared and gone, and nothing around it now but a soft wide spread of yaller velvet, which was the sand.

That was the right place to stop, and we done it. We set there a-looking and a-thinking for a half an hour, nobody a-saying anything, for it made us feel quiet and kind of solemn to remember it had been looking out over that valley just that same way, and thinking its awful thoughts all to itself for thousands of years, and nobody can't find out what they are to this day.

At last I took up the glass and see some little black things a-capering around on that velvet carpet, and some more a-climbing up the cretur's back, and then I see two or three little wee puffs of white smoke, and told Tom to look. He done it, and says—

"They're bugs. No—hold on; they—why, I believe they're men. Yes, it's men—men and horses, both. They're hauling a long ladder up onto the Sphinx's back—now ain't that odd? And now they're trying to lean it up a—there's some more puffs of smoke—it's guns! Huck, they're after Jim!"

We clapped on the power, and went for them a-biling. We was there in no time, and come a-whizzing down amongst them, and they broke and scattered every which way, and some that was climbing the ladder after Jim let go all holts and fell. We soared up and found him laying on top of the head panting and most tuckered out, partly from howling for help and partly from scare. He had been standing a siege a long time—a week, *he* said, but it warn't so, it only just seemed so to him because they was crowding him so. They had shot at him, and rained the bullets all around him, but he warn't hit, and when they found he wouldn't stand up and the bullets couldn't git at him when he was laying down, they went for the ladder, and then he knowed it was all up with him if we didn't come pretty quick. Tom was very indignant, and asked him why he didn't show the flag and command them to *git*, in the name of the United States. Jim said he done it, but they never paid no attention. Tom said he would have this thing looked into at Washington, and says—

"You'll see that they'll have to apologize for insulting the flag, and pay an indemnity, too, on top of it, even if they git off *that* easy."

Jim says—

"What's an indemnity, Mars Tom?"

"It's cash, that's what it is."

"Who gits it, Mars Tom?"

"Why, *we* do."

"En who gits de apology?"

"The United States. Or, we can take whichever we please. We can take the apology, if we want to, and let the gov'ment take the money."

"How much money will it be, Mars Tom?"

"Well, in an aggravated case like this one, it will be at least three dollars apiece, and I don't know but more."

"Well, den, we'll take de money, Mars Tom, blame de 'pology. Hain't dat yo' notion, too? En hain't it yourn, Huck?"

JIM STANDING A SIEGE.

We talked it over a little and allowed that that was as good a way as any, so we agreed to take the money. It was a new business to me, and I asked Tom if countries always apologized when they had done wrong, and he says—

"Yes; the little ones does."

We was sailing around examining the Pyramids, you know, and now we soared up and roosted on the flat top of the biggest one, and found it was just like what the man said in the Sunday school. It was like four pairs of stairs that starts broad at the bottom and slants up and comes together in a point at the top, only these stair-steps couldn't be clumb the way you climb other stairs; no, for each step was as high as your chin, and you have to be boosted up from behind. The two other Pyramids warn't far away, and the people moving about on the sand between looked like bugs crawling, we was so high above them.

Tom he couldn't hold himself he was so worked up with gladness and astonishment to be in such a celebrated place, and he just dripped history from every pore, seemed to me. He said he couldn't scarcely believe he was standing on the very identical spot the prince flew from on the Bronze Horse. It was in the Arabian Night times, he said. Somebody give the prince a bronze horse with a peg in its shoulder, and he could git on him and fly through the air like a bird, and go all over the world, and steer it by turning the peg, and fly high or low and land wherever he wanted to.

When he got done telling it there was one of them uncomfortable silences that comes, you know, when a person has been telling a whopper and you feel sorry for him and wish you could think of some way to change the subject and let him down easy, but git stuck and don't see no way, and before you can pull your mind together and *do* something, that silence has got in and spread itself and done the business. I was embarrassed, Jim he was embarrassed, and neither of us couldn't say a word. Well, Tom he glowered at me a minute, and says—

"Come, out with it. What do you think?"

I says—

"Tom Sawyer, *you* don't believe that, yourself."

"What's the reason I don't? What's to hender me?"

"There's one thing to hender you: it couldn't happen, that's all."

"What's the reason it couldn't happen?"

"You tell me the reason it *could* happen."

"This balloon is a good enough reason it could happen, I should reckon."

"*Why* is it?"

"*Why* is it? I never saw such an idiot. Ain't this balloon and the bronze horse the same thing under different names?"

"No, they're not. One is a balloon and the other's a horse. It's very different. Next you'll be saying a house and a cow is the same thing."

"By Jackson, Huck's got him agin! Dey ain't no wigglin' outer dat!"

"Shut your head, Jim; you don't know what you're talking about. And Huck don't. Look here, Huck, I'll make it plain to you, so you can understand. You see, it ain't the mere *form* that's got anything to do with their being similar or unsimilar, it's the *principle* involved; and the principle is the same in both. Don't you see, now?"

I turned it over in my mind, and says—

"Tom, it ain't no use. Principles is all very well, but they don't git around that one big fact, that the thing that a balloon can do ain't no sort of proof of what a horse can do."

RESCUE OF JIM.

"Shucks, Huck, you don't get the idea at all. Now look here a minute—it's perfectly plain. Don't we fly through the air?"

"Yes."

"Very well. Don't we fly high or fly low, just as we please?"

"Yes."

"Don't we steer whichever way we want to?"

"Yes."

"And don't we land when and where we please?"

"Yes."

"How do we move the balloon and steer it?"

"By touching the buttons."

"*Now* I reckon the thing is clear to you at last. In the other case the moving and steering was done by turning a peg. We touch a button, the prince turned a peg. There ain't an atom of difference, you see. I knowed I could git it through your head if I stuck to it long enough."

He felt so happy he begun to whistle. But me and Jim was silent, so he broke off surprised, and says—

"Looky here, Huck Finn, don't you see it *yet?*"

I says—

"Tom Sawyer, I want to ask you some questions."

"Go ahead," he says, and I see Jim chirk up to listen.

"As I understand it, the whole thing is in the buttons and the peg—the rest ain't of no consequence. A button is one shape, a peg is another shape, but that ain't any matter?"

"No, that ain't any matter, as long as they've both got the same power."

"All right, then. What is the power that's in a candle and in a match?"

"It's the fire."

"It's the same in both, then?"

"Yes, just the same in both."

"All right. Suppose I set fire to a carpenter shop with a match, what will happen to that carpenter shop?"

"She'll burn up."

"And suppose I set fire to this Pyramid with a candle—will she burn up?"

"Of course she won't."

"All right. Now the fire's the same, both times. *Why* does the shop burn, and the Pyramid don't?"

"Because the Pyramid *can't* burn."

"Aha! and *a horse can't fly!*"

"My lan', ef Huck ain't got him agin! Huck's landed him high en dry dis time, *I* tell you! Hit's de smartes' trap I ever see a body walk inter—en ef I—"

But Jim was so full of laugh he got to strangling and couldn't go on, and Tom was that mad to see how neat I had floored him, and turned his own argument agin him and knocked him all to rags and flinders with it that all he could manage to say was that whenever he heard me and Jim try to argue it made him ashamed of the human race. I never said nothing, I was feeling pretty well satisfied. When I have got the best of a person that way, it ain't my way to go around crowing about it the way some people does, for I consider that if I was in his place I wouldn't wish him to crow over me. It's better to be generous, that's what I think.

CHAPTER 13

BY AND BY we left Jim to float around up there in the neighborhood of the Pyramids, and we clumb down to the hole where you go into the tunnel, and went in with some Arabs and candles, and away in there in the middle of the Pyramid we found a room and a big stone box in it where they used to keep that king, just as the man in the Sunday school said, but he was gone, now, somebody had got him. But I didn't take no interest in the place, because there could be ghosts there, of course; not fresh ones, but I don't like no kind.

So then we come out and got some little donkeys and rode a piece, and then went in a boat another piece, and then more donkeys, and got to Cairo; and all the way the road was as smooth and beautiful a road as ever I see, and had tall date pams on both sides, and naked children everywhere, and the men was as red as copper, and fine and strong and handsome. And the city was a curiosity. Such narrow streets—why, they were just lanes, and crowded with people with turbans, and women with veils, and everybody rigged out in blazing bright clothes and all sorts of colors, and you wondered how the camels and the people got by each other in such narrow little cracks, but they done it—a perfect jam, you see, and everybody noisy. The stores warn't big enough to turn around in, but you didn't have to go in; the storekeeper sat tailor fashion on his counter, smoking his snaky long pipe, and had his things where he could reach them to sell, and he was just as good as in the street, for the camel-loads brushed him as they went by.

Now and then a grand person flew by in a carriage with fancy dressed men running and yelling in front of it and whacking anybody with a long rod that didn't get out of the way. And by and by along comes the Sultan riding horseback at the head of a procession, and fairly took your breath away his clothes was so splendid; and everybody fell flat and laid on his stomach while he went by. I forgot, but a feller helped me remember. He was one that had a rod and run in front.

There was churches, but they don't know enough to keep Sunday, they keep Friday and break the Sabbath. You have to take off your shoes when you go in. There was crowds of men and boys in the church, setting in groups on the stone floor and making no end of noise—getting their lessons by heart, Tom said, out of the Koran, which they think is a Bible, and people that knows better knows enough to not let on. I never see such a big church in my life before, and most awful high, it was; it made you dizzy to look up; our village church at home ain't a circumstance to it; if you was to put it in there, people would think it was a dry-goods box.

What I wanted to see was a dervish, because I was interested in dervishes on accounts of the one that played the trick on the camel driver. So we found a lot in a kind of a church, and they called themselves Whirling Dervishes; and they did whirl, too, I never see anything like it. They had tall sugar-loaf hats on, and linen petticoats; and they spun and spun and spun, round and round like tops, and the petticoats stood out on a slant, and it was the prettiest thing I ever see, and made me drunk to look at it. They was all Moslems, Tom said, and when I asked him what a Moslem was, he said it was a person that wasn't a Presbyterian. So there is plenty of them in Missouri, though I didn't know it before.

We didn't see half there was to see in Cairo, because Tom was in such a sweat to hunt out places that was celebrated in history. We had a most tiresome time to find the granary where Joseph stored up the grain before the famine, and when we found it it warn't worth much to look at, being such an old tumble-down wreck, but Tom was sat-isfied, and made more fuss over it than I would make if I stuck a nail in my foot. How he ever found that place was too many for me. We passed as much as forty just like it before we come to it, and any of them would a done for me, but none but just the right one would suit him; I never see anybody so particular as Tom Sawyer. The minute he struck the right one he reconnized it as easy as I would reconnize my other shirt if I had one, but how he done it he couldn't any more tell than he could fly; he said so himself.

Then we hunted a long time for the house where the boy lived that learned the cadi how to try the case of the old olives and the new ones, and said it was out of the Arabian Nights and he would tell me and Jim about it when he got time. Well, we hunted and hunted till I was ready to drop, and I wanted Tom to give it up and come next day and git somebody that knowed the town and could talk Missourian and could go straight to the place; but no, he wanted to find it himself, and nothing else would answer. So on we went. Then at last the remarkablest thing happened I ever see. The house was gone—gone hundreds of years ago—every last rag of it gone but just one mud brick. Now a person wouldn't ever believe that a backwoods Missouri boy that hadn't ever been in that town before could go and hunt that place over and find that brick, but Tom Sawyer done it. I know he done it, because I see him do it. I was right by his very side at the time, and see him see the brick and see him reconnize it. Well, I says to myself, how *does* he do it? is it knowledge, or is it instink?

Now there's the facts, just as they happened: let everybody explain it their own way. I've ciphered over it a good deal, and it's my opinion that some of it is knowledge but the main bulk of it is instink. The reason is this. Tom put the brick in his pocket to give to a museum with his name on it and the facts when he went home, and I slipped it out and put another brick considerable like it in its place, and he didn't know the difference—but there was a difference, you see. I think that settles it—it's mostly instink, not knowledge. Instink tells him where the exact *place* is for the brick to be in, and so he reconnizes it by the place it's in, not by the look of the brick. If it was knowledge, not instink, he would know the brick again by the look of it the next time he seen it—which he didn't. So it shows that for all the brag you hear about knowledge being such a wonderful thing, instink is worth forty of it for real unerringness. Jim says the same.

When we got back Jim dropped down and took us in, and there was a young man there with a red skull cap and tassel on and a beautiful blue silk jacket and baggy trousers with a shawl around his waist and pistols in it that could talk English and wanted to hire to us as guide and take us to Mecca and Medina and Central Africa and everywheres for a half a dollar a day and his keep, and we hired him and left, and piled on the power, and by the time we was through dinner we was over the place where the Israelites crossed the Red Sea when Pharaoh tried to overtake them and was caught by the waters. We stopped, then, and had a good look at the place, and it done Jim good to see it.

He said he could see it all, now, just the way it happened; he could see
the Israelites walking along between the walls of water, and the Egyp-
tians coming, from away off yonder, hurrying all they could, and see
them start in as the Israelites went out, and then, when they was all in,
see the walls tumble together and drown the last man of them. Then
we piled on the power again and rushed away and huvvered over
Mount Sinai, and saw the place where Moses broke the tables of stone,
and where the children of Israel camped in the plain and worshiped
the golden calf, and it was all just as interesting as could be, and the
guide knowed every place as well as I know the village at home.

But we had an accident, now, and it fetched all the plans to a
standstill. Tom's old ornery corn-cob pipe had got so old and swelled
and warped that she couldn't hold together any longer, notwithstand-
ing the strings and bandages, but caved in and went to pieces. Tom he
didn't know *what* to do. The Professor's pipe wouldn't answer, it
warn't anything but a mershum, and a person that's got used to a cob
pipe knows it lays a long ways over all the other pipes in this world, and
you can't git him to smoke any other. He wouldn't take mine, I
couldn't persuade him. So there he was.

He thought it over, and said we must scour around and see if we
could roust out one in Egypt or Arabia or around in some of these
countries, but the guide said no, it warn't no use, they didn't have
them. So Tom was pretty glum for a little while, then he chirked up
and said he'd got the idea and knowed what to do. He says—

"I've got another corn-cob pipe, and it's a prime one, too, and nearly
new. It's laying on the rafter that's right over the kitchen stove at home
in the village. Jim, you and the guide will go and get it, and me and
Huck will camp here on Mount Sinai till you come back."

"But Mars Tom, we couldn't ever find de village. I could find de
pipe, 'caze I knows de kitchen, but my lan', *we* can't ever find de
village, nur Sent Louis, nur none o' dem places. We don't know de way,
Mars Tom."

That was a fact, and it stumped Tom for a minute. Then he said—

"Looky here, it can be done, sure; and I'll tell you how. You set your
compass and sail west as straight as a dart, till you find the United
States. It ain't any trouble, because it's the first land you'll strike, the
other side of the Atlantic. If it's daytime when you strike it, bulge right
on, straight west from the upper part of the Florida coast, and in an

hour and three quarters you'll hit the mouth of the Mississippi—at the speed that I'm going to send you. You'll be so high up in the air that the earth will be curved considerable—sorter like a washbowl turned upside down—and you'll see a raft of rivers crawling around every which way, long before you get there, and you can pick out the Mississippi without any trouble. Then you can follow the river north nearly an hour and three quarters, till you see the Ohio come in; then you want to look sharp, because you're getting near. Away up to your left you'll see another thread coming in—that's the Missouri and is a little above St. Louis. You'll come down low, then, so as you can examine the villages as you spin along. You'll pass about twenty-five in the next fifteen minutes, and you'll reconnize ours when you see it—and if you don't, you can yell down and ask."

"Ef it's dat easy, Mars Tom, I reckon we kin do it—yassir, I knows we kin."

The guide was sure of it, too, and thought that he could learn to stand his watch in a little while.

"Jim can learn you the whole thing in a half an hour," Tom said. "This balloon's as easy to manage as a canoe."

Tom got out the chart and marked out the course and measured it, and says—

"To go back west is the shortest way, you see. It's only about seven thousand miles. If you went east, and so on around, it's over twice as far." Then he says to the guide, "I want you both to watch the tell-tale all through the watches, and whenever it don't mark three hundred miles an hour, you go higher or drop lower till you find a storm-current that's going your way. There's a hundred miles an hour in this old thing without any wind to help. There's two-hundred-mile gales to be found, any time you want to hunt for them."

"We'll hunt for them, sir."

"See that you do. Sometimes you may have to go up a couple of miles, and it 'll be pison cold, but most of the time you'll find your storm a good deal lower. If you can only strike a cyclone—that's the ticket for you! You'll see by the Professor's books that they travel west in these latitudes; and they travel low, too."

Then he ciphered on the time and says—

"Seven thousand miles, three hundred miles an hour—you can make the trip in a day—twenty-four hours. This is Thursday; you'll be back here Saturday afternoon. Come, now, hustle out some blankets and food and books and things for me and Huck, and you can start right along. There ain't no occasion to fool around—I want a smoke, and the quicker you fetch that pipe the better."

All hands jumped for the things, and in eight minutes our things was out and the balloon was ready for America. So we shook hands good-bye, and Tom give his last orders:

"It's 10 minutes to 2 p.m., now, Mount Sinai time. In 24 hours you'll be home, and it 'll be 6 to-morrow morning, village time. When you strike the village, land a little back of the top of the hill, in the woods, out of sight; then you rush down, Jim, and shove these letters in the post office, and if you see anybody stirring, pull your slouch down over your face so they won't know you. Then you go and slip in the back way, to the kitchen and git the pipe, and lay this piece of paper on the kitchen table and put something on it to hold it, and then slide out and git away and don't let Aunt Polly catch a sight of you, nor nobody else. Then you jump for the balloon and shove for Mount Sinai three hundred miles an hour. You won't have lost more than an hour. You'll start back at 7 or 8 a.m., village time, and be here in 24 hours, arriving at 2 or 3 p.m., Mount Sinai time."

Tom he read the piece of paper to us. He had wrote on it—

"THURSDAY AFTERNOON. *Tom Sawyer the Erronort sends his love to Aunt Polly from* MOUNT SINAI *where the Ark was, and so does Huck Finn and she will get it to-morrow morning half past six.**

"TOM SAWYER THE ERRONORT."

"That 'll make her eyes bug out and the tears come," he says. Then he says—

"Stand by! One—two—three—away you go!"

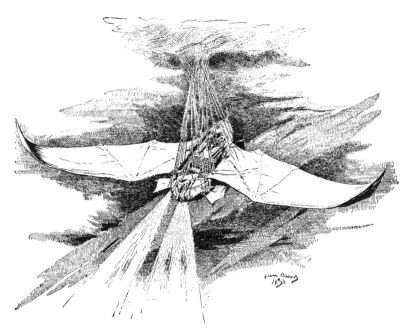

HOMEWARD BOUND.

And away she *did* go! Why, she seemed to whiz out of sight in a second.

Then we found a most comfortable cave that looked out over that whole big plain, and there we camped to wait for the pipe.

The balloon come back all right, and brung the pipe; but Aunt Polly

---

*This misplacing of the Ark is probably Huck's error, not Tom's.—M.T.

had catched Jim when he was getting it, and anybody can guess what happened: she sent for Tom. So Jim he says—

"Mars Tom, she's out on de porch wid her eye sot on de sky a-layin' for you, en she say she ain't gwyne to budge from dah tell she gits hold of you. Dey's gwyne to be trouble, Mars Tom, 'deed dey is."

So then we shoved for home, and not feeling very gay, neither.

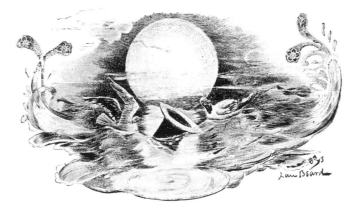

MARK TWAIN

TOM SAWYER, DETECTIVE

Tom Sawyer, Detective

AS TOLD BY HUCK FINN

CHAPTER 1

WELL, IT WAS the next spring after me and Tom Sawyer set our old nigger Jim free the time he was chained up for a runaway slave down there on Tom's uncle Silas's farm in Arkansaw. The frost was working out of the ground and out of the air, too, and it was getting closer and closer onto barefoot time every day; and next it would be marble time, and next mumbletypeg, and next tops and hoops, and next kites, and then right away it would be summer and going in a-swimming. It just makes a boy homesick to look ahead like that and see how far off summer is. Yes, and it sets him to sighing and saddening around, and there's something the matter with him, he don't know what. But anyway, he gets out by himself and mopes and thinks; and mostly he hunts for a lonesome place high up on the hill in the edge of the woods and sets there and looks away off on the big Mississippi down there a-reaching miles and miles around the points where the timber looks smoky and dim it's so fur off and still, and everything's so solemn it seems like everybody you've loved is dead and gone and you most wish you was dead and gone too, and done with it all.

Don't you know what that is? It's spring fever. That is what the name of it is. And when you've got it, you want—oh, you don't quite know what it is you *do* want, but it just fairly makes your heart ache, you want it so! It seems to you that mainly what you want is, to get away;

get away from the same old tedious things you're so used to seeing and so tired of, and see something new. That is the idea; you want to go and be a wanderer; you want to go wandering far away to strange countries where everything is mysterious and wonderful and romantic. And if you can't do that, you'll put up with considerable less; you'll go anywhere you *can* go, just so as to get away, and be thankful of the chance, too.

Well, me and Tom Sawyer had the spring fever, and had it bad, too; but it warn't any use to think about Tom trying to get away, because, as he said, his aunt Polly wouldn't let him quit school and go trapsing off somers wasting time; so we was pretty blue. We was setting on the front steps one day about sundown talking this way, when out comes his aunt Polly with a letter in her hand and says—

"Tom, I reckon you've got to pack up and go down to Arkansaw —your aunt Sally wants you."

I most jumped out of my skin for joy. I reckoned Tom would fly at his aunt and hug her head off; but if you will believe me he set there like a rock, and never said a word. It made me fit to cry to see him act so foolish, with such a noble chance as this opening up. Why, we might lose it if he didn't speak up and show he was thankful and grateful. But he set there and studied and studied till I was that distressed I didn't know what to do; then he says, very ca'm—and I could a shot him for it:

"Well," he says, "I'm right down sorry, aunt Polly, but I reckon I got to be excused—for the present."

His aunt Polly was knocked so stupid and so mad at the cold impudence of it, that she couldn't say a word for as much as a half a minute, and this give me a chance to nudge Tom and whisper:

"Ain't you got any sense? Sp'iling such a noble chance as this and throwing it away?"

But he warn't disturbed. He mumbled back:

"Huck Finn, do you want me to let her *see* how bad I want to go? Why, she'd begin to doubt, right away, and imagine a lot of sicknesses and dangers and objections, and first you know she'd take it all back. You lemme alone; I reckon I know how to work her."

Now I never would a thought of that. But he was right. Tom Sawyer was always right—the levelest head I ever see, and always *at* himself and ready for anything you might spring on him. By this time his aunt Polly was all straight again, and she let fly. She says:

"You'll be excused! *You* will! Well, I never heard the like of it in all my days! The idea of you talking like that to *me*! Now take yourself off and pack your traps; and if I hear another word out of you about what you'll be excused from and what you won't, I lay *I'll* excuse you—with a hickory!"

She hit his head a thump with her thimble as we dodged by, and he let on to be whimpering as we struck for the stairs. Up in his room he hugged me, he was so out of his head for gladness because we was going traveling. And he says:

"Before we get away she'll wish she hadn't let me go, but she won't know any way to get around it, now. After what she's said, her pride won't let her take it back."

Tom was packed in ten minutes, all except what his aunt and Mary would finish up for him; then we waited ten more for her to get cooled down and sweet and gentle again; for Tom said it took her ten minutes to

"I RECKON I GOT TO BE EXCUSED."

unruffle in times when half of her feathers was up, but twenty when they was all up, and this was one of the times when they was all up. Then we went down, being in a sweat to know what the letter said.

She was setting there in a brown study, with it laying in her lap. We set down, and she says:

"They're in considerable trouble down there, and they think you and Huck'll be a kind of a diversion for them—'comfort,' they say. Much of that they'll get out of you and Huck Finn, I reckon. There's a neighbor named Brace Dunlap that's been wanting to marry their Benny for three months, and at last they told him pine blank and once for all, he *couldn't*; so he has soured on them and they're worried about it. I reckon he's somebody they think they better be on the good side of, for they've tried to please him by hiring his no-account brother to help on the farm when they can't hardly afford it and don't want him around anyhow. Who are the Dunlaps?"

"They live about a mile from uncle Silas's place, aunt Polly,—all the farmers live about a mile apart, down there—and Brace Dunlap is a long sight richer than any of the others, and owns a whole grist of niggers. He's a widower thirty-six years old, without any children, and is proud of his money and overbearing, and everybody is a little afraid of him, and knuckles down to him and tries to keep on the good side of him. I judge he thought he could have any girl he wanted, just for the asking, and it must have set him back a good deal when he found he couldn't get Benny. Why, Benny's only half as old as he is, and just as sweet and lovely as—well, you've seen her. Poor old uncle Silas—why, it's pitiful, him trying to curry favor that way—so hard pushed and poor, and yet hiring that useless Jubiter Dunlap to please his ornery brother."

"What a name—Jubiter! Where'd he get it?"

"It's only just a nickname. I reckon they've forgot his real name long before this. He's twenty-seven, now, and has had it ever since the first time he ever went in swimming. The school teacher seen a round brown mole the size of a dime on his left leg above his knee and four little bits of moles around it, when he was naked, and he said it minded him of Jubiter and his moons; and the children thought it was funny, and so they got to calling him Jubiter, and he's Jubiter yet. He's tall, and lazy, and sly, and sneaky, and ruther cowardly, too, but kind of good natured, and wears long brown hair and no beard, and hasn't got a cent, and Brace boards him for nothing, and gives him his old clothes to wear, and despises him. Jubiter is a twin."

"What's t'other twin like?"

"Just exactly like Jubiter—so they say; used to was, anyway, but he hain't been seen for seven years. He got to robbing, when he was nineteen or twenty, and they jailed him; but he broke jail and got away—up North here, somers. They used to hear about him robbing and burglaring now and then, but that was years ago. He's dead, now. At least that's what they say. They don't hear about him any more."

"What was his name?"

"Jake."

There wasn't anything more said for a considerable while; the old lady was thinking. At last she says:

"The thing that is mostly worrying your aunt Sally is the tempers that that man Jubiter gets your uncle into."

Tom was astonished, and so was I. Tom says:

"Tempers? Uncle Silas? Land, you must be joking! I didn't know he *had* any temper."

"Works him up into perfect rages, your aunt Sally says; says he acts as if he would really hit the man, sometimes."

"Aunt Polly, it beats anything I ever heard of. Why, he's just as gentle as mush."

"Well, she's worried, anyway. Says your uncle Silas is like a changed man, on account of all this quarreling. And the neighbors talk about it, and lay all the blame on your uncle, of course, because he's a preacher and hain't got any business to quarrel. Your aunt Sally says he hates to go into the pulpit he's so ashamed; and the people have begun to get cool towards him, and he ain't as popular now as he used to was."

"Well, ain't it strange? Why, aunt Polly, he was always so good and kind and moony and absent-minded and chuckle-headed and lovable—why, he was just an angel! What *can* be the matter of him, do you reckon?"

CHAPTER 2

WE HAD POWERFUL good luck; because we got a chance in a sternwheeler from away North which was bound for one of them bayous or one-horse rivers away down Louisiana-way, and so we could go all the way down the Upper Mississippi and all the way down the Lower Mississippi to that farm in Arkansaw without having to change steamboats at St. Louis: not so very much short of a thousand miles at one pull.

A pretty lonesome boat; there warn't but few passengers, and all old folks, that set around, wide apart, dozing, and was very quiet. We was four days getting out of the "upper river," because we got aground so much. But it warn't dull—couldn't be for boys that was traveling, of course.

From the very start me and Tom allowed that there was somebody sick in the stateroom next to ourn, because the meals was always toted in there by the waiters. By and by we asked about it—Tom did—and the waiter said it was a man, but he didn't look sick.

"Well, but *ain't* he sick?"

"I don't know; maybe he is, but 'pears to me he's jest letting on."

"What makes you think that?"

"Because if he was sick he would pull his clothes off *some* time or other, don't you reckon he would? Well, this one don't. At least he don't ever pull off his boots, anyway."

"The mischief he don't! Not even when he goes to bed?"

"No."

It was always nuts for Tom Sawyer—a mystery was. If you'd lay out a mystery and a pie before me and him, you wouldn't have to say take your choice, it was a thing that would regulate itself. Because in my nature I have always run to pie, whilst in his nature he has always run to mystery. People are made different. And it is the best way. Tom says to the waiter:

"What's the man's name?"

"Phillips."

"Where'd he come aboard?"

"I think he got aboard at Elexandria, up on the Iowa line."

"What do you reckon he's a-playing?"

"I hain't any notion—I never thought of it."

I says to myself, here's another one that runs to pie.

"Anything peculiar about him?—the way he acts or talks?"

"No—nothing, except he seems so scary, and keeps his doors locked night and day both, and when you knock he won't let you in till he opens the door a crack and sees who it is."

"By jimminy, it's intresting! I'd like to get a look at him. Say—the next time you're going in there, don't you reckon you could spread the door and—"

"No indeedy! He's always behind it. He would block that game."

Tom studied over it, and then he says:

"Looky-here. You lend me your apern and let me take him his breakfast in the morning. I'll give you a quarter."

The boy was plenty willing enough, if the head steward wouldn't mind. Tom says that's all right, he reckoned he could fix it with the head steward; and he done it. He fixed it so as we could both go in with aperns on and toting vittles.

He didn't sleep much, he was in such a sweat to get in there and find out the mystery about Phillips; and moreover he done a lot of guessing about it all night, which warn't no use, for if you are going to find out the facts of a thing, what's the sense in guessing out what ain't the facts and wasting ammunition? I didn't lose no sleep. I wouldn't give a dern to know what's the matter of Phillips, I says to myself.

Well, in the morning we put on the aperns and got a couple of trays of truck, and Tom he knocked on the door. The man opened it a crack, and then he let us in and shut it quick. By Jackson, when we got a sight of him we most dropped the trays! and Tom says:

"Why, Jubiter Dunlap, where'd *you* come from!"

Well, the man was astonished, of course; and first-off he looked like he didn't know whether to be scared, or glad, or both, or which, but finally he settled down to being glad; and then his color come back, though at first his face had turned pretty white. So we got to talking together while he et his breakfast. And he says:

"But I ain't Jubiter Dunlap. I'd just as soon tell you who I am, though, if you'll swear to keep mum, for I ain't no Phillips, either."

Tom says:

"We'll keep mum, but there ain't any need to tell who you are if you ain't Jubiter Dunlap."

"Why?"

"Because if you ain't him you're t'other twin, Jake. You're the spit'n image of Jubiter."

"Well, I *am* Jake. But looky-here, how do you come to know us Dunlaps?"

Tom told about the adventures we'd had down there at his uncle Silas's last summer; and when he see that there warn't anything about his folks,—or him either, for that matter—that we didn't know, he opened out and talked perfectly free and candid. He never made any bones about his own case; said he'd been a hard lot, was a hard lot yet, and reckoned he'd *be* a hard lot plum to the end. He said of course it was a dangersome life, and—

He give a kind of a gasp, and set his head like a person that's listening. We didn't say anything, and so it was very still for a second or so and there warn't no sounds but the screaking of the woodwork and the chug-chugging of the machinery down below.

Then we got him comfortable again, telling him about his people, and how Brace's wife had been dead three years, and Brace wanted to marry Benny and she shook him, and Jubiter was working for uncle Silas, and him and uncle Silas quarreling all the time—and then he let go and laughed.

"Land!" he says, "it's like old times to hear all this tittle-tattle, and does me good. It's been seven years and more since I heard any. How do they talk about me these days?"

"Who?"

"The farmers—and the family."

"Why, they don't talk about you at all—at least only just a mention, once in a long time."

"The nation!" he says, surprised, "why is that?"

"Because they think you are dead long ago."

"No! Are you speaking true?—honor bright, now." He jumped up, excited.

"Honor bright. There ain't anybody thinks you are alive."

"Then I'm saved—I'm saved, sure! I'll go home. They'll hide me and save my life. You keep mum. Swear you'll keep mum—swear you'll

"SWEAR YOU'LL BE GOOD TO ME AND HELP ME SAVE MY LIFE!"

never, never tell on me. Oh, boys, be good to a poor devil that's being hunted day and night, and dasn't show his face! I've never done you any harm—I'll never do you any, as God is in the heavens—swear you'll be good to me and help me save my life!"

We'd a swore it if he'd been a dog; and so we done it. Well, he couldn't love us enough for it or be grateful enough, poor cuss; it was all he could do to keep from hugging us.

We talked along, and he got out a little handbag and begun to open it, and told us to turn our backs. We done it, and when he told us to turn again he was perfectly different to what he was before. He had on blue goggles and the naturalest-looking long brown whiskers and mustashers you ever see. His own mother wouldn't a knowed him. He asked us if he looked like his brother Jubiter, now.

"No," Tom said, "there ain't anything left that's like him except the long hair."

"All right, I'll get that cropped close to my head before I get there;

then him and Brace will keep my secret, and I'll live with them as being a stranger and the neighbors won't ever guess me out. What do you think?"

Tom he studied a while, then he says:

"Well, of course me and Huck are going to keep mum there, but if you don't keep mum yourself there's going to be a little bit of a risk—it

"SOUNDED LIKE COCKING A GUN!"

ain't much, maybe, but it's a little. I mean, if you talk won't people notice that your voice is just like Jubiter's, and mightn't it make them think of the twin they reckoned was dead but maybe after all was hid all this time under another name?"

"By George," he says, "you're a sharp one! You're perfectly right. I've got to play deef and dumb when there's a neighbor around. If I'd a struck for home and forgot that little detail— However, I wasn't striking for home. I was breaking for any place where I could get away from these fellows that are after me; then I was going to put on this disguise and get some different clothes and—"

He jumped for the outside door and laid his ear against it and listened, pale and kind of panting. Presently he whispers—

"Sounded like cocking a gun! Lord what a life to lead!"

Then he sunk down in a chair all limp and sick-like, and wiped the sweat off of his face.

CHAPTER 3

FROM THAT TIME OUT, we was with him most all the time, and one
or t'other of us slept in his upper berth. He said he had been so
lonesome, and it was such a comfort to him to have company, and
somebody to talk to in his troubles. We was in a sweat to find out what
his secret was, but Tom said the best way was not to seem anxious,
then likely he would drop into it himself in one of his talks, but if we
got to asking questions he would get suspicious and shet up his shell.
It turned out just so. It warn't no trouble to see that he *wanted* to talk
about it, but always along at first he would scare away from it when he
got on the very edge of it, and go to talking about something else. At
last he come out with it, though. The way it come about, was this. He
got to asking us, kind of indifferent-like, about the passengers down on
deck. We told him about them. But he warn't satisfied; we warn't
particular enough. He told us to describe them better. Tom done it. At
last, when Tom was describing one of the roughest and raggedest ones,
he give a shiver and a gasp and says:

"Oh, lordy, that's one of them! They're aboard sure—I just knowed
it. I sort of hoped I had got away, but I never believed it. Go on."

Presently when Tom was describing another mangy rough deck
passenger, he give that shiver again and says—

"That's him!—that's the other one. If it would only come a good
black stormy night and I could get ashore! You see, they've got spies on
me. They've got a right to come up and buy drinks at the bar yonder
forrard, and they take that chance to bribe somebody to keep watch on
me—porter or boots or somebody. If I was to slip ashore without
anybody seeing me they would know it inside of an hour."

So then he got to wandering along and pretty soon, sure enough, he
was telling! He was poking along through his ups and downs, and when
he come to that place he went right along. He says:

"It was a confidence-game. We played it on a julery shop in St. Louis.

What we was after was a couple of noble big di'monds as big as hazelnuts, which everybody was running to see. We was dressed up fine, and we played it on them in broad daylight. We ordered the di'monds sent to the hotel for us to see if we wanted to buy, and when we was examining them we had paste counterfeits all ready, and *them* was the things that went back to the shop when we said the water wasn't quite fine enough for twelve thousand dollars."

"Twelve—thousand—dollars!" Tom says. "Was they really worth all that money, do you reckon?"

"Every cent of it."

"And you fellows got away with them?"

"As easy as nothing. I don't reckon the julery people know they've been robbed, yet. But it wouldn't be good sense to stay around St. Louis, of course, so we considered where we'd go. One was for going one way, one another; so we throwed up heads or tails and the upper Mississippi won. We done up the di'monds in a paper and put our names on it and put it in the keep of the hotel clerk and told him not to ever let either of us have it again without the others was on hand to see it done; then we went down town, each by his own self—because I reckon maybe we all had the same notion. I don't know for certain, but I reckon maybe we had."

"What notion?" Tom says.

"To rob the others."

"What—one take everything, after all of you had helped to get it?"

"Cert'nly."

It disgusted Tom Sawyer, and he said it was the orneriest low-downest thing he ever heard of. But Jake Dunlap said it warn't unusual in the profession. Said when a person was in that line of business he'd got to look out for his own intrust, there warn't nobody else going to do it for him. And then he went on. He says:

"You see, the trouble was, you couldn't divide up two di'monds amongst three. If there'd been three—but never mind about that, there *warn't* three. I loafed along the back streets studying and studying. And I says to myself, I'll hog them di'monds the first chance I get, and I'll have a disguise all ready, and I'll give the boys the slip, and when I'm safe away I'll put it on, and then let them find me if they can. So I got the false whiskers and the goggles and this countrified suit of clothes, and fetched them along back in a hand-bag; and when I was

passing a shop where they sell all sorts of things, I got a glimpse of one
of my pals through the window. It was Bud Dixon. I was glad, you bet.
I says to myself, I'll see what he buys. So I kept shady, and watched.
Now what do you reckon it was he bought?"

"Whiskers?" says I.

"No."

"Goggles?"

"No."

"Oh, keep still, Huck Finn, can't you; you're only just hendering, all
you can. What *was* it he bought, Jake?"

"You'd never guess in the world. It was only just a screw-driver—just
a wee little bit of a screw-driver."

"Well, I declare! What did he want with that?"

"That's what *I* thought. It was curious. It clean stumped me. I says to
myself, what can he want with that thing? Well, when he come out I
stood back out of sight and then tracked him to a second-hand slop-
shop and see him buy a red flannel shirt and some old ragged clothes
—just the ones he's got on now, as you've described. Then I went
down to the wharf and hid my things aboard the up-river boat that we
had picked out, and then started back and had another streak of luck.
I seen our other pal lay in *his* stock of old rusty second-handers. We got
the di'monds and went aboard the boat.

"But now we was up a stump, for we couldn't go to bed. We had to
set up and watch one another. Pity, that was; pity to put that kind of a
strain on us, because there was bad blood between us from a couple of
weeks back, and we was only friends in the way of business. Bad
anyway, seeing there was only two di'monds betwixt three men. First
we had supper, and then tramped up and down the deck together
smoking till most midnight, then we went and set down in my
stateroom and locked the doors and looked in the piece of paper to
see if the di'monds was all right, then laid it on the lower berth right in
full sight; and there we set, and set, and by and by it got to be dreadful
hard to keep awake. At last Bud Dixon he dropped off. As soon as he
was snoring a good regular gait that was likely to last, and had his chin
on his breast and looked permanent, Hal Clayton nodded towards the
di'monds and then towards the outside door, and I understood. I
reached and got the paper, and then we stood up and waited perfectly
still; Bud never stirred; I turned the key of the outside door very soft

"WE STOOD UP AND WAITED PERFECTLY STILL."

and slow, then turned the knob the same way and we went tip-toeing out onto the guard and shut the door very soft and gentle.

"There warn't nobody stirring, anywhere, and the boat was slipping along, swift and steady, through the big water in the smoky moonlight. We never said a word, but went straight up onto the hurricane deck and plum back aft and set down on the end of the skylight. Both of us knowed what that meant, without having to explain to one another. Bud Dixon would wake up and miss the swag, and would come straight for us, for he ain't afeard of anything or anybody, that man ain't. He would come, and we would heave him overboard, or get killed trying. It made me shiver, because I ain't as brave as some people, but if I showed the white feather—well, I knowed better than do that. I kind of hoped the boat would land somers and we could skip ashore and not have to run the risk of this row, I was so scared of Bud Dixon, but she was an upper-river tub and there warn't no real chance of that.

"Well, the time strung along and along, and that feller never come! Why, it strung along till dawn begun to break, and still he never come. 'Thunder,' I says, 'what do you make out of this?—ain't it suspicious?' 'Land!' Hal says, 'do you reckon he's playing us?—open the paper!' I done it, and by gracious there warn't anything in it but a couple of little pieces of loaf sugar! *That's* the reason he could set there and snooze all night so comfortable. Smart? Well, I reckon! He had had them two papers all fixed and ready, and he had put one of them in place of t'other right under our noses.

"We felt pretty cheap. But the thing to do, straight off, was to make a plan; and we done it. We would do up the paper again, just as it was, and slip in, very elaborate and soft, and lay it on the bunk again and let on *we* didn't know about any trick and hadn't any idea he was a-laughing at us behind them bogus snores of his'n; and we would stick by him, and the first night we was ashore we would get him drunk and search him, and get the di'monds; and *do* for him, too, if it warn't too risky. If we got the swag, we'd *got* to do for him, or he would hunt us down and do for us, sure. But I didn't have no real hope. I knowed we could get him drunk,—he was always ready for that—but what's the good of it? You might search him a year and never find—

"Well, right there I catched my breath and broke off my thought! For an idea went ripping through my head that tore my brains to rags—and land, but I felt gay and good! You see, I had had my boots off, to unswell my feet, and just then I took up one of them to put it on, and I catched a glimpse of the heel-bottom, and it just took my breath away. You remember about that puzzlesome little screw-driver?"

"You bet I do," says Tom, all excited.

"Well, when I catched that glimpse of that boot-heel, the idea that went smashing through my head was, *I* know where he's hid the di'monds! You look at this boot-heel, now. See, it's bottomed with a steel plate, and the plate is fastened on with little screws. Now there wasn't a screw about that feller anywhere but in his boot-heels; so, if he needed a screw-driver I reckoned I knowed why."

"Huck, ain't it bully!" says Tom.

"Well, I got my boots on and we went down and slipped in and laid the paper of sugar on the berth and set down soft and sheepish and went to listening to Bud Dixon snore. Hal Clayton dropped off pretty soon, but I didn't; I wasn't ever so wide awake in my life. I was spying out from under the shade of my hat brim, searching the floor for leather. It took me a long time, and I begun to think maybe my guess was wrong, but at last I struck it. It laid over by the bulkhead, and was nearly the color of the carpet. It was a little round plug about as thick as the end of your little finger, and I says to myself there's a di'mond in the nest you've come from. Before long I spied out the plug's mate.

"Think of the smartness and the coolness of that blatherskite! He put up that scheme on us and reasoned out what we would do, and we went ahead and done it perfectly exact, like a couple of pudd'nheads. He set there and took his own time to unscrew his heel-plates and cut out his plugs and stick in the di'monds and screw on his plates again. He allowed we would steal the bogus swag and wait all night for him to come up and get drownded, and by George it's just what we done! *I* think it was powerful smart."

"You bet your life it was!" says Tom, just full of admiration.

CHAPTER 4

Well, all day we went through the humbug of watching one another, and it was pretty sickly business for two of us and hard to act out, I can tell you. About night we landed at one of them little Missouri towns high up towards Iowa, and had supper at the tavern, and got a room up stairs with a cot and a double bed in it, but I dumped my bag under a deal table in the dark hall whilst we was moving along it to bed, single file, me last, and the landlord in the lead with a tallow candle. We had up a lot of whisky and went to playing high-low-jack for dimes, and as soon as the whisky begun to take hold of Bud we stopped drinking but we didn't let him stop. We loaded him till he fell out of his chair and laid there snoring.

"We was ready for business, now. I said we better pull our boots off, and his'n too, and not make any noise, then we could pull him and haul him around and ransack him without any trouble. So we done it. I set my boots and Bud's side by side, where they'd be handy. Then we stripped him and searched his seams and his pockets and his socks and the inside of his boots, and everything, and searched his bundle. Never found any di'monds. We found the screw-driver, and Hal says, 'What do you reckon he wanted with that?' I said I didn't know; but when he wasn't looking I hooked it. At last Hal he looked beat and discouraged and said we'd got to give it up. That was what I was waiting for. I says:

" 'There's one place we hain't searched.'

" 'What place is that?' he says.

" 'His stomach.'

" 'By gracious, I never thought of that! *Now* we're on the home stretch, to a dead moral certainty. How'll we manage?'

" 'Well,' I says, 'just stay by him till I turn out and hunt up a drug store and I reckon I'll fetch something that'll make them di'monds tired of the company they're keeping.'

"He said that's the ticket, and with him looking straight at me I slid

"SEARCHED HIS SEAMS AND HIS POCKETS AND HIS SOCKS."

myself into Bud's boots instead of my own, and he never noticed. They
was just a shade large for me, but that was considerable better than
being too small. I got my bag as I went a-groping through the hall, and
in about a minute I was out the back way and stretching up the river
road at a five-mile gait.

"And not feeling so very bad, neither—walking on di'monds don't
have no such effect. When I had gone fifteen minutes I says to myself
there's more'n a mile behind me and everything quiet. Another five
minutes and I says there's considerable more land behind me now, and
there's a man back there that's begun to wonder what's the trouble.
Another five and I says to myself he's getting real uneasy—he's walking the floor, now. Another five, and I says to myself, there's two mile
and a half behind me, and he's *awful* uneasy—beginning to cuss, I
reckon. Pretty soon I says to myself, forty minutes gone—he *knows*

there's something up! Fifty minutes—the truth's a-busting on him, now! he is reckoning I found the di'monds whilst we was searching, and shoved them in my pocket and never let on—yes, and he's starting out to hunt for me. He'll hunt for new tracks in the dust, and they'll as likely send him down the river as up.

"Just then I see a man coming down on a mule, and before I thought I jumped into the bush. It was stupid! When he got abreast he stopped and waited a little for me to come out; then he rode on again. But I didn't feel gay any more. I says to myself I've botched my chances by that; I surely have, if he meets up with Hal Clayton.

"Well, about three in the morning I fetched Elexandria and see this sternwheeler laying there and was very glad, because I felt perfectly safe, now, you know. It was just daybreak. I went aboard and got this stateroom and put on these clothes and went up in the pilot house—to watch, though I didn't reckon there was any need of it. I set there and played with my di'monds and waited and waited for the boat to start, but she didn't. You see, they was mending her machinery, but I didn't know anything about it, not being very much used to steamboats.

"Well, to cut the tale short, we never left there till plum noon; and long before that I was hid in this stateroom; for before breakfast I see a man coming, away off, that had a gait like Hal Clayton's, and it made me just sick. I says to myself, it's him, sure. If he finds out I'm aboard this boat, he's got me like a rat in a trap. All he's got to do is to have me watched, and wait—wait till I slip ashore, thinking he is a thousand miles away, then slip after me and dog me to a good place and make me give up the di'monds, and then he'll—oh, *I* know what he'll do! Ain't it awful—awful! And now to think the *other* one's aboard, too! Oh, ain't it hard luck, boys—ain't it hard! But you'll help save me, *won't* you?—oh, boys, be good to a poor devil that's being hunted to death, and save me—I'll worship the very ground you walk on!"

We turned in and soothed him down and told him we would plan for him and help him and he needn't be so afeard; and so, by and by he got to feeling kind of comfortable again, and unscrewed his heel-plates and held up his di'monds this way and that admiring them and loving them; and when the light struck into them they *was* beautiful, sure; why they seemed to kind of bust, and snap fire out all around. But all the same I judged he was a fool. If I had been him I would 'a' handed the di'monds to them pals and got them to go ashore and leave me alone. But he was made different. He said it was a whole fortune and he couldn't bear the idea.

Twice we stopped to fix the machinery and laid a good while, once in the night; but it wasn't dark enough and he was afeard to skip. But the third time we had to fix it there was a better chance. We laid up at a country woodyard about forty mile above uncle Silas's place a little after one at night, and it was thickening up and going to storm. So Jake he laid for a chance to slide. We begun to take in wood. Pretty soon the rain come a-drenching down, and the wind blowed hard. Of course every boat-hand fixed a gunny sack and put it on like a bonnet the way they do when they are toting wood and we got one for Jake and he slipped down aft with his hand-bag and come tramping forrard in the rank of men, and he looked just like the rest, and walked ashore with them and when we see him pass out of the light of the torch-basket and get swallowed up in the dark we got our breath again and just felt grateful and splendid. But it wasn't for long. Somebody told, I reckon; for in about eight or ten minutes them two pals come tearing forrard as tight as they could jump, and darted ashore and was gone. We waited plum till dawn for them to come back, and kept hoping they would, but they never did. We was awful sorry and low spirited. All the hope we had was, that Jake had got such a start that they couldn't

"WALKED ASHORE."

get on his track and he would get to his brother's and hide there and be safe.

He was going to take the river road, and told us to find out if Brace and Jubiter was to home and no strangers there, and then slip out about sundown and tell him. Said he would wait for us in a little bunch of sycamores right back of Tom's uncle Silas's tobacker field, on the river road, a lonesome place.

We set and talked a long time about his chances, and Tom said he was all right if the pals struck up the river instead of down, but it wasn't likely, because maybe they knowed where he was from; more likely they would go right, and dog him all day, him not suspecting, and kill him when it come dark and take the boots. So we was pretty sorrowful.

CHAPTER 5

We DIDN'T GET DONE tinkering the machinery till away late in the afternoon, and so it was so close to sundown when we got home that we never stopped on our road but made a break for the sycamores as tight as we could go, to tell Jake what the delay was, and have him wait till we could go to Brace's and find out how things was, there. It was getting pretty dim by the time we turned the corner of the woods, sweating and panting with that long run, and see the sycamores thirty yards ahead of us; and just then we see a couple of men run into the bunch and heard two or three terrible screams for help. "Poor Jake is killed, sure," we says. We was scared through and through, and broke for the tobacker field and hid there, trembling so our clothes would hardly stay on; and just as we skipped in there a couple of men went tearing by, and into the bunch they went, and in a second out jumps four men and took out up the road as tight as they could go, two chasing two.

We laid down, kind of weak and sick, and listened for more sounds, but didn't hear none, for a good while, but just our hearts. We was thinking of that awful thing laying yonder in the sycamores, and it seemed like being that close to a ghost, and it give me the cold shudders. The moon come a-swelling up out of the ground, now, powerful big and round and bright, behind a comb of trees, like a face looking through prison bars, and the black shadders and white places begun to creep around and it was miserable quiet and still and night-breezy and grave-yardy and scary. All of a sudden Tom whispers:

"Look!—what's that?"

"Don't!" I says. "Don't take a person by surprise that way. I'm most ready to die, anyway, without you doing that."

"Look, I tell you. It's something coming out of the sycamores."

"*Don't*, Tom!"

"It's terrible tall!"

"Oh, lordy-lordy! let's—"

"Keep still—it's a-coming this way."

He was so excited he could hardly get breath enough to whisper. I had to look, I couldn't help it. So now we was both on our knees with our chins on a fence-rail and gazing—Yes, and gasping, too. It was coming down the road—coming in the shadder of the trees, and you couldn't see it good; not till it was pretty close to us; then it stepped into a bright splotch of moonlight and we sunk right down in our tracks—it was Jake Dunlap's ghost! That was what we said to ourselves.

We couldn't stir for a minute or two; then it was gone. We talked about it in low voices. Tom says:

"They're mostly dim and smoky, or like they're made out of fog, but this one wasn't."

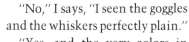

"No," I says, "I seen the goggles and the whiskers perfectly plain."

"Yes, and the very colors in them loud countrified Sunday clothes—plaid breeches, green and black—"

"Cotton-velvet westcot, fire-red and yaller squares—"

"Leather straps to the bottoms of the breeches-legs and one of them hanging unbuttoned—"

"Yes, and that hat—"

"What a hat for a ghost to wear!"

You see it was the first season anybody wore that kind—a black stiff-brim stove-pipe, very high, and not smooth, with a round top—just like a sugar-loaf.

"Did you notice if its hair was the same, Huck?"

"IT WAS JAKE DUNLAP'S GHOST!"

"No—seems to me I did, then again it seems to me I didn't."

"I didn't either, but it had its bag along, I noticed that."

"So did I. How can there be a ghost-bag, Tom?"

"Sho! I wouldn't be as ignorant as that if I was you, Huck Finn. Whatever a ghost has, turns to ghost-stuff. They've got to have their things, like anybody else. You see, yourself, that its clothes was turned to ghost-stuff. Well, then, what's to hender its bag from turning, too? Of course it done it."

That was reasonable. I couldn't find no fault with it. Bill Withers and his brother Jack come along by, talking, and Jack says:

"What do you reckon it was he was toting?"

"I dunno; but it was pretty heavy."

"Yes, all he could lug. Nigger stealing corn from old parson Silas, I judged."

"So did I. And so I allowed I wouldn't let on to see him."

"That's me, too!"

Then they both laughed, and went on out of hearing. It showed how unpopular old uncle Silas had got to be, now. They wouldn't 'a' let a nigger steal anybody else's corn and never done anything to him.

We heard some more voices mumbling along towards us and getting louder, and sometimes a cackle of a laugh. It was Lem Beebe and Jim Lane. Jim Lane says:

"Who?—Jubiter Dunlap?"

"Yes."

"Oh, I don't know. I reckon so. I seen him spading up some ground along about an hour ago, just before sundown—him and the parson. Said he guessed he wouldn't go to-night, but we could have his dog if we wanted him."

"Too tired, I reckon."

"Yes—works so hard!"

"Oh, you bet!"

They cackled at that, and went on by. Tom said we better jump out and tag along after them, because they was going our way and it wouldn't be comfortable to run across the ghost all by ourselves. So we done it, and got home all right.

That night was the second of September—a Saturday. I shan't ever forget it. You'll see why, pretty soon.

CHAPTER 6

WE TRAMPED ALONG behind Jim and Lem till we come to the back stile where old Jim's cabin was that he was captivated in, the time we set him free, and here come the dogs piling around us to say howdy, and there was the lights of the house, too; so we warn't afeard, any more, and was going to climb over, but Tom says:

"Hold on; set down here a minute. By George!"

"What's the matter?" says I.

"Matter enough!" he says. "Wasn't you expecting we would be the first to tell the family who it is that's been killed yonder in the sycamores, and all about them rapscallions that done it, and about the di'monds they've smouched off of the corpse, and paint it up fine and have the glory of being the ones that knows a lot more about it than anybody else?"

"Why, of course. It wouldn't be you, Tom Sawyer, if you was to let such a chance go by. I reckon it ain't going to suffer none for lack of paint," I says, "when you start in to scollop the facts."

"Well, now," he says, perfectly ca'm, "what would you say if I was to tell you I ain't going to start in at all?"

I was astonished to hear him talk so. I says:

"I'd say it's a lie. You ain't in earnest, Tom Sawyer."

"You'll soon see. Was the ghost barefooted?"

"No it wasn't. What of it?"

"You wait—I'll show you what. Did it have its boots on?"

"Yes. I seen them plain."

"Swear it?"

"Yes, I swear it."

"So do I. Now do you know what that means?"

"No. What does it mean?"

"Means that them thieves *didn't get the di'monds!*"

"Jimminy! What makes you think that?"

"I don't only think it, I know it. Didn't the breeches and goggles and whiskers and hand-bag and every blessed thing turn to ghost-stuff? Everything it had on turned, didn't it? It shows that the reason its boots turned, too, was because it still had them on after it started to go ha'nting around, and if that ain't proof that them blatherskites didn't get the boots I'd like to know what you'd *call* proof."

"WAS THE GHOST BAREFOOTED?"

Think of that, now. I never see such a head as that boy had. Why *I* had eyes and I could see things, but they never meant nothing to me. But Tom Sawyer was different. When Tom Sawyer seen a thing it just got up on its hind legs and *talked* to him—told him everything it knowed. *I* never see such a head.

"Tom Sawyer," I says, "I'll say it again as I've said it a many a time before: I ain't fitten to black your boots. But that's all right—that's neither here nor there. God Amighty made us all, and some He gives eyes that's blind, and some He gives eyes that can see, and I reckon it ain't none of our lookout what He done it for; it's all right, or He'd a fixed it some other way. Go on—I see plenty plain enough, now, that them thieves didn't get away with the di'monds. Why didn't they, do you reckon?"

"Because they got chased away by them other two men before they could pull the boots off of the corpse."

"*That's* so! I see it now. But looky-here, Tom, why ain't we to go and tell about it?"

"Oh, shucks, Huck Finn, can't you see? Look at it. What's a-going to happen? There's going to be an inquest in the morning. Them two men will tell how they heard the yells and rushed there just in time to not save the stranger. Then the jury 'll twaddle and twaddle and twaddle, and finally they'll fetch in a verdict that he got shot or stuck or busted over the head with something, and come to his death by the inspiration of God. And after they've buried him they'll auction off his things for to pay the expenses, and then's *our* chance."

"How, Tom?"

"Buy the boots for two dollars!"

Well, it most took my breath.

"My land! Why Tom, *we'll* get the di'monds!"

"You bet. Some day there'll be a big reward offered for them—a thousand dollars, sure. That's our money! Now we'll trot in and see the folks. And mind you we don't know anything about any murder, or any di'monds, or any thieves—don't you forget that."

I had to sigh a little over the way he had got it fixed. I'd a *sold* them di'monds—yes, sir, for twelve thousand dollars; but I didn't say anything. It wouldn't done any good. I says:

"But what are we going to tell your aunt Sally has made us so long getting down here from the village, Tom?"

"Oh, I'll leave that to you," he says. "I reckon you can explain it somehow."

He was always just that strict and delicate. He never would tell a lie himself.

We struck across the big yard, noticing this, that and t'other thing that was so familiar, and we so glad to see it again; and when we got to the roofed big passageway betwixt the double log house and the kitchen part, there was everything hanging on the wall just as it used to was, even to uncle Silas's old faded green baize working-gown with the hood to it and the raggedy white patch between the shoulders that always looked like somebody had hit him with a snowball; and then we lifted the latch and walked in. Aunt Sally she was just a-ripping and a-tearing around, and the children was huddled in one corner and the old man he was huddled in the other and praying for help in time of need. She jumped for us with joy and tears running down her face and give us a whacking box on the ear, and then hugged us and kissed us and boxed us again, and just couldn't seem to get enough of it she was so glad to see us; and she says:

"Where *have* ye been a-loafing to, you good-for-nothing trash! I've been that worried about ye I didn't know what to do. Your traps has been here *ever* so long, and I've had supper cooked fresh about four times so as to have it hot and good when you come, till at last my patience is just plum wore out, and I declare I—I—why I could skin you alive! You must be starving, poor things!—set down, set down, everybody, don't lose no more time."

It was mighty good to be there again behind all that noble corn pone and spare-ribs and everything that you could ever want in this world. Old uncle Silas he peeled off one of his bulliest old-time blessings, with as many layers to it as an onion, and whilst the angels was hauling in the slack of it I was trying to study up what to say about what kept us so long. When our plates was all loadened and we'd got a-going, she asked me and I says:

"Well, you see,—er—Mizzes—"

"Huck Finn! Since when am I Mizzes to you? Have I ever been stingy of cuffs or kisses for you since the day you stood in this room and I took you for Tom Sawyer and blessed God for sending you to me, though you told me four thousand lies and I believed every one of them like a simpleton? Call me aunt Sally—like you always done."

So I done it. And I says:

"Well, me and Tom allowed we would come along afoot and take a smell of the woods, and we run across Lem Beebe and Jim Lane and they asked us to go with them blackberrying to-night, and said they could borrow Jubiter Dunlap's dog, because he had told them just that minute—"

"Where did they see him?" says the old man; and when I looked up to see how *he* come to take an intrust in a little thing like that, his eyes was just burning into me he was that eager. It surprised me so it kind of throwed me off, but I pulled myself together again and says:

"It was when he was spading up some ground along with you, towards sundown or along there."

He only just said "Um," in a kind of a disappointed way, and didn't take no more intrust. So I went on. I says:

"Well then, as I was a-saying—"

"That'll do, you needn't go no furder." It was aunt Sally. She was boring right into me with her eyes, and very indignant. "Huck Finn," she says, "how'd them men come to talk about going a-blackberrying in September—in *this* region?"

I see I had slipped up, and I couldn't say a word. She waited, still a-gazing at me, then she says:

"And how'd they come to strike that idiot idea of going a-blackberrying in the night?"

"Well m'm, they—er—they told us they had a lantern, and—"

"Oh, *shet* up—do! Looky-here; what was they going to do with a dog?—hunt blackberries with it?"

"I think, m'm, they—."

"Now, Tom Sawyer, what kind of a lie are you fixing *your* mouth to contribit to this mess of rubbage? Speak out—and I warn you before you begin, that I don't believe a word of it. You and Huck's been up to something you no business to—*I* know it perfectly well; *I* know you, *both* of you. Now you explain that dog, and them blackberries, and the lantern, and the rest of that rot—and mind you talk as straight as a string—do you hear?"

Tom he looked considerable hurt, and says, very dignified:

"It is a pity if Huck is to be talked to thataway, just for making a little bit of a mistake that anybody could make."

"What mistake has he made?"

"Why, only the mistake of saying blackberries when of course he meant strawberries."

"Tom Sawyer, I lay if you aggravate me a little more, I'll—"

"Aunt Sally, without knowing it—and of course without intending it—you are in the wrong. If you'd 'a' studied natural history the way you ought, you would know that all over the world except just here in Arkansaw they *always* hunt strawberries with a dog—and a lantern—"

But she busted in on him there and just piled into him and snowed him under. She was so mad she couldn't get the words out fast enough, and she gushed them out in one everlasting freshet. That was what Tom Sawyer was after. He allowed to work her up and get her started and then leave her alone and let her burn herself out. Then she would be so aggravated with that subject that she wouldn't say another word about it nor let anybody else. Well, it happened just so. When she was tuckered out and had to hold up, he says, quite ca'm:

"And yet, all the same, aunt Sally—"

"Shet up!" she says, "I don't want to hear another word out of you."

So we was perfectly safe, then, and didn't have no more trouble about that delay. Tom done it elegant.

CHAPTER 7

Benny she was looking pretty sober, and she sighed some, now and then; but pretty soon she got to asking about Mary, and Sid, and Tom's aunt Polly, and then aunt Sally's clouds cleared off and she got in a good humor and joined in on the questions and was her lovingest best self, and so the rest of the supper went along gay and pleasant. But the old man he didn't take any hand hardly, and was absent-minded and restless, and done a considerable amount of sighing; and it was kind of heart-breaking to see him so sad and troubled and worried.

By and by, a spell after supper, come a nigger and knocked on the door and put his head in with his old straw hat in his hand bowing and scraping, and said his Marse Brace was out at the stile and wanted his brother, and was getting tired waiting supper for him, and would Marse Silas please tell him where he was? I never see uncle Silas speak up so sharp and fractious before. He says:

"Am *I* his brother's keeper?" And then he kind of wilted together, and looked like he wished he hadn't spoke so, and then he says, very gentle: "But you needn't say that, Billy; I was took sudden and irritable, and I ain't very well these days, and not hardly responsible. Tell him he ain't here."

And when the nigger was gone he got up and walked the floor, backwards and forrards and backwards and forrards, mumbling and muttering to himself and plowing his hands through his hair. It was real pitiful to see him. Aunt Sally she whispered to us and told us not to take notice of him, it embarrassed him. She said he was always thinking and thinking, since these troubles come on, and she allowed he didn't more'n about half know what he was about when the thinking spells was on him; and she said he walked in his sleep considerable more now than he used to, and sometimes wandered around over the house and even out doors in his sleep, and if we catched him at it we must let him alone and not disturb him. She said she reckoned it didn't do him no harm, and maybe it done him good. She said Benny was the only one that was much help to him these days. Said Benny appeared to know just when to try to soothe him and when to leave him alone.

So he kept on tramping up and down the floor and muttering, till by and by he begun to look pretty tired; then Benny she went and snuggled up to his side and put one hand in his and one arm around his waist and walked with him; and he smiled down on her, and reached down and kissed her; and so, little by little the trouble went out of his face and she persuaded him off to his room. They had very pretty petting ways together, and it was uncommon pretty to see.

Aunt Sally she was busy getting the children ready for bed; so by and by it got dull and tedious, and me and Tom took a turn in the moonlight, and fetched up in the watermelon patch and et one, and had a good deal of talk. And Tom said he'd bet the quarreling was all Jubiter's fault, and he was going to be on hand the first time he got a chance, and see; and if it was so, he was going to do his level best to get uncle Silas to turn him off.

And so we talked and smoked and stuffed watermelon as much as two hours, and then it was pretty late, and when we got back the house was quiet and dark and everybody gone to bed.

Tom he always seen everything, and now he see that the old green baize work-gown was gone, and said it wasn't gone when we went out; and so we allowed it was curious, and then we went up to bed.

We could hear Benny stirring around in her room, which was next to ourn, and judged she was worried a good deal about her father and couldn't sleep. We found we couldn't, neither. So we set up a long time and smoked and talked in a low voice, and felt pretty dull and downhearted. We talked the murder and the ghost over and over again, and got so creepy and crawly we couldn't get sleepy no how and no way.

By and by, when it was away late in the night and all the sounds was late sounds and solemn, Tom nudged me and whispers to me to look, and I done it, and there we see a man poking around in the yard like he didn't know just what he wanted to do, but it was pretty dim and we couldn't see him good. Then he started for the stile, and as he went over it the moon come out strong and he had a long-handled shovel over his shoulder and we see the white patch on the old work-gown. So Tom says:

"SMOKED AND STUFFED WATERMELON."

"He's a-walking in his sleep. I wish we was allowed to follow him and see where he's going to. There, he's turned down by the tobacker field. Out of sight, now. It's a dreadful pity he can't rest no better."

We waited a long time, but he didn't come back any more, or if he did he come around the other way; so at last we was tuckered out and went to sleep and had nightmares, a million of them. But before dawn we was awake again, because meantime a storm had come up and been raging, and the thunder and lightning was awful and the wind was a-thrashing the trees around and the rain was driving down in slanting sheets, and the gullies was running rivers. Tom says:

"Looky-here, Huck, I'll tell you one thing that's mighty curious. Up to the time we went out, last night, the family hadn't heard about Jake Dunlap being murdered. Now the men that chased Hal Clayton and Bud Dixon away would spread the thing around in a half an hour, and every neighbor that heard it would shin out and fly around from one farm to t'other and try to be the first to tell the news. Land, they don't have such a big thing as that to tell twice in thirty year! Huck, it's mighty strange; I don't understand it."

So then he was in a fidget for the rain to let up, so we could turn out and run across some of the people and see if they would say anything about it to us. And he said if they did we must be horribly surprised and shocked.

We was out and gone the minute the rain stopped. It was just broad day, then. We loafed along up the road, and now and then met a person and stopped and said howdy, and told them when we come, and how we left the folks at home, and how long we was going to stay, and all that, but none of them said a word about that thing—which was just astonishing, and no mistake. Tom said he believed if we went to the sycamores we would find that body laying there solitary and alone and not a soul around. Said he believed the men chased the thieves so far into the woods that the thieves prob'ly seen a good chance and turned on them at last, and maybe they all killed each other and so there wasn't anybody left to tell.

First we knowed, gabbling along thataway, we was right at the sycamores. The cold chills trickled down my back and I wouldn't budge another step, for all Tom's persuading. But he couldn't hold in; he'd got to see if the boots was safe on that body yet. So he crope in—and the next minute out he come again with his eyes bulging he was so excited, and says:

"Huck, it's gone!"

I was astonished! I says:

"Tom, you don't mean it."

"It's gone, sure. There ain't a sign of it. The ground is trompled some, but if there was any blood it's all washed away by the storm, for it's all puddles and slush in there."

At last I give in, and went and took a look myself; and it was just as Tom said—there wasn't a sign of a corpse.

"Dern it," I says, "the di'monds is gone. Don't you reckon the thieves slunk back and lugged him off, Tom?"

"Looks like it. It just does. Now where'd they hide him, do you reckon?"

"I don't know," I says, disgusted, "and what's more I don't care. They've got the boots, and that's all I cared about. He'll lay around these woods a long time before I hunt him up."

Tom didn't feel no more intrust in him neither, only curiosity to know what come of him; but he said we'd lay low and keep dark and it wouldn't be long till the dogs or somebody rousted him out.

We went back home to breakfast ever so bothered and put out and disappointed and swindled. I warn't ever so down on a corpse before.

"HUCK, IT'S GONE!"

CHAPTER 8

IT WARN'T VERY CHEERFUL at breakfast. Aunt Sally she looked old and tired and let the children snarl and fuss at one another and didn't seem to notice it was going on, which wasn't her usual style; me and Tom had a plenty to think about without talking; Benny she looked like she hadn't had much sleep, and whenever she'd lift her head a little and steal a look towards her father you could see there was tears in her eyes; and as for the old man his things stayed on his plate and got cold without him knowing they was there, I reckon, for he was thinking and thinking all the time, and never said a word and never et a bite.

By and by when it was stillest, that nigger's head was poked in at the door again, and he said his Marse Brace was getting powerful uneasy about Marse Jubiter, which hadn't come home yet, and would Marse Silas please—

He was looking at uncle Silas, and he stopped there, like the rest of his words was froze; for uncle Silas he rose up shaky and steadied himself leaning his fingers on the table, and he was panting, and his eyes was set on the nigger, and he kept swallowing, and put his other hand up to his throat a couple of times, and at last he got his words started, and says:

"Does he—does he—think—*what* does he think! Tell him—tell him—" Then he sunk down in his chair limp and weak, and says, so as you could hardly hear him: "Go away—go away!"

The nigger looked scared, and cleared out, and we all felt—well I don't know how we felt, but it was awful, with the old man panting there, and his eyes set and looking like a person that was dying. None of us could budge; but Benny she slid around soft, with her tears running down, and stood by his side, and nestled his old gray head up against her and begun to stroke it and pet it with her hands, and nodded to us to go away, and we done it, going out very quiet, like the dead was there.

Me and Tom struck out for the woods mighty solemn, and saying how different it was now to what it was last summer when we was here and everything was so peaceful and happy and everybody thought so much of uncle Silas, and he was so cheerful and simple-hearted and pudd'nheaded and good—and now look at him. If he hadn't lost his mind he wasn't much short of it. That was what we allowed.

It was a most lovely day, now, and bright and sunshiny; and the further and further we went over the hill towards the prairie the lovelier and lovelier the trees and flowers got to be and the more it seemed strange and somehow wrong that there had to be trouble in such a world as this. And then all of a sudden I catched my breath and grabbed Tom's arm, and all my livers and lungs and things fell down into my legs.

"There it is!" I says. We jumped back behind a bush shivering, and Tom says:

"'Sh!—don't make a noise."

"*WHAT* DOES HE THINK!"

It was setting on a log right in the edge of the little prairie, thinking. I tried to get Tom to come away, but he wouldn't, and I dasn't budge by myself. He said we mightn't ever get another chance to see one, and he was going to look his fill at this one if he died for it. So I looked too, though it give me the fan-tods to do it. Tom he *had* to talk, but he talked low. He says:

"Poor Jakey, it's got all its things on, just as he said he would. *Now* you see what we wasn't certain about—its hair. It's not long, now, the way it was; it's got it cropped close to its head, the way he said he would. Huck, I never see anything look any more naturaler than what It does."

"Nor I neither," I says; "I'd reconnize it anywheres."

"So would I. It looks perfectly solid and genuwyne, just the way it done before it died."

So we kept a-gazing. Pretty soon Tom says:

"Huck, there's something mighty curious about this one; don't you know that? *It* oughtn't to be going around in the daytime."

"That's so, Tom—I never heard the like of it before."

"No, sir, they don't ever come out only at night—and then not till after twelve. There's something wrong about this one, now you mark my words. I don't believe it's got any right to be around in the daytime. But don't it look natural! Jake said he was going to play deef and dumb here, so the neighbors wouldn't know his voice. Do you reckon it would do that if we was to holler at it?"

"Lordy, Tom, don't talk so! If you was to holler at it I'd die in my tracks."

"Don't you worry, I ain't going to holler at it. Look, Huck, it's a-scratching its head—don't you see?"

"Well, what of it?"

"Why, this. What's the sense of it scratching its head? There ain't anything there to itch; its head is made out of fog or something like that, and *can't* itch. A fog can't itch; any fool knows that."

"Well, then, if it don't itch and can't itch, what in the nation is it scratching it for? Ain't it just habit, don't you reckon?"

"No, sir, I don't. I ain't a bit satisfied about the way this one acts. I've a blame good notion it's a bogus one—I have, as sure as I'm a-setting here. Because, if it—Huck!"

"Well, what's the matter now?"

"You can't see the bushes through it!"

"Why, Tom, it's so, sure! It's as solid as a cow. I sort of begin to think—"

"Huck, it's biting off a chaw of tobacker! By George *they* don't chaw—they hain't got anything to chaw *with*. Huck!"

"I'm a-listening."

"It ain't a ghost at all. It's Jake Dunlap his own self!"

"Oh, your granny!" I says.

"Huck Finn, did we find any corpse in the sycamores?"

"No."

"Or any sign of one?"

"No."

"Mighty good reason. Hadn't ever been any corpse there."

"Why Tom, you know we heard—"

"Yes, we did—heard a howl or two. Does that prove anybody was killed? Course it don't. And we seen four men run, then this one come walking out and we took it for a ghost. No more ghost than you are. It was Jake Dunlap his own self, and it's Jake Dunlap now. He's been and got his hair cropped, the way he said he would, and he's playing himself for a stranger, just the same as he said he would. Ghost! Him?—he's as sound as a nut."

Then I see it all, and how we had took too much for granted. I was powerful glad he didn't get killed, and so was Tom, and we wondered which he would like the best—for us to never let on to know him, or how? Tom reckoned the best way would be to go and ask him. So he started; but I kept a little behind, because I didn't know but it might be a ghost, after all. When Tom got to where he was, he says:

"Me and Huck's mighty glad to see you again, and you needn't be afeard we'll tell. And if you think it'll be safer for you if we don't ever let on to know you when we run across you, say the word and you'll see you can depend on us and would ruther cut our hands off than get you into the least little bit of danger."

First-off he looked surprised to see us, and not very glad, either; but as Tom went on he looked pleasanter, and when he was done he smiled, and nodded his head several times, and made signs with his hands, and says:

"Goo-goo,—goo-goo," the way deef and dummies does.

Just then we see some of Steve Nickerson's people coming that lived t'other side of the prairie, so Tom says:

"GOO-GOO,—GOO-GOO."

"You do it elegant; I never see anybody do it better. You're right: play it on us, too; play it on us same as the others; it'll keep you in practice and prevent you making blunders. We'll keep away from you and let on we don't know you, but any time we can be any help, you just let us know."

Then we loafed along past the Nickersons, and of course they asked if that was the new stranger yonder, and where'd he come from, and what was his name, and which communion was he, Babtis or Methodis, and which politics, whig or democrat, and how long is he staying, and all them other questions that humans always asks when a stranger comes, and dogs does too. But Tom said he warn't able to make anything out of deef and dumb signs, and the same with goo-gooing.

Then we watched them go and bullyrag Jake; because we was pretty uneasy for him. Tom said it would take him days to get so he wouldn't forget he was a deef and dummy sometimes, and speak out before he thought. When we had watched long enough to see that Jake was getting along all right and working his signs very good, we loafed along again, allowing to strike the school-house about recess time, which was a three-mile tramp.

I was so disappointed not to hear Jake tell about the row in the sycamores and how near he come to getting killed, that I couldn't seem to get over it; and Tom he felt the same, but said if we was in Jake's fix we would want to go careful and keep still and not take any chances.

The boys and girls was all glad to see us again, and we had a real good time all through recess. Coming to school the Henderson boys had come across the new deef and dummy and told the rest; so all the scholars was chuck full of him and couldn't talk about anything else, and was in a sweat to get a sight of him because they hadn't ever seen a deef and dummy in their lives, and it made a powerful excitement.

Tom said it was tough to have to keep mum now; said we would be heroes if we could come out and tell all we knowed; but after all it was still more heroic to keep mum, there warn't two boys in a million could do it. That was Tom Sawyer's idea about it, and I reckoned there warn't anybody could better it.

CHAPTER 9

In the next two or three days Dummy he got to be powerful popular. He went associating around with the neighbors, and they made much of him and was proud to have such a rattling curiosity amongst them. They had him to breakfast, they had him to dinner, they had him to supper; they kept him loaded up with hog and hominy, and warn't ever tired staring at him and wondering over him, and wishing they knowed more about him he was so uncommon and romantic. His signs warn't no good; people couldn't understand them and he prob'ly couldn't himself, but he done a sight of goo-gooing, and so everybody was satisfied, and admired to hear him go it. He toted a piece of slate around, and a pencil; and people wrote questions on it and he wrote answers; but there warn't anybody could read his writing but Brace Dunlap. Brace said he couldn't read it very good, but he could manage to dig out the meaning most of the time. He said Dummy said he belonged away off somers, and used to be well off but got busted by swindlers which he had trusted, and was poor now, and hadn't any way to make a living.

Everybody praised Brace Dunlap for being so good to that stranger. He let him have a little log cabin all to himself, and had his niggers take care of it and fetch him all the vittles he wanted.

Dummy was at our house some, because old uncle Silas was so afflicted himself, these days, that anybody else that was afflicted was a comfort to him. Me and Tom didn't let on that we had knowed him before, and he didn't let on that he had knowed us before. The family talked their troubles out before him the same as if he wasn't there, but we reckoned it wasn't any harm for him to hear what they said. Generly he didn't seem to notice, but sometimes he did.

Well, two or three days went along, and everybody got to getting uneasy about Jubiter Dunlap. Everybody was asking everybody if they had any idea what had become of him. No, they hadn't, they said; and they shook their heads and said there was something powerful strange about it. Another and another day went by; then there was a report got around that praps he was murdered. You bet it made a big stir! Everybody's tongue was clacking away after that. Saturday two or three gangs turned out and hunted the woods to see if they could run across his remainders. Me and Tom helped, and it was noble good times and exciting. Tom he was so brim full of it he couldn't eat nor rest. He said if we could find that corpse we would be celebrated, and more talked about than if we got drownded.

The others got tired and give it up; but not Tom Sawyer—that warn't his style. Saturday night he didn't sleep any, hardly, trying to think up a plan; and towards daylight in the morning he struck it. He snaked me out of bed and was all excited, and says—

"Quick, Huck, snatch on your clothes—I've got it! Bloodhound!"

In two minutes we was tearing up the river road in the dark towards the village. Old Jeff Hooker had a bloodhound and Tom was going to borrow him. I says—

"The trail's too old, Tom—and besides, it's rained, you know."

"It don't make any difference, Huck. If the body's hid in the woods anywhere around, the hound will find it. If he's been murdered and buried, they wouldn't bury him deep, it ain't likely, and if the dog goes over the spot he'll scent him, sure. Huck, we're going to be celebrated, sure as you're born!"

He was just a-blazing; and whenever he got afire he was most likely to get afire all over. That was the way this time. In two minutes he had got it all ciphered out, and wasn't only just going to find the corpse —no, he was going to get on the track of that murderer and hunt *him* down, too; and not only that, but he was going to stick to him till—

"Well," I says, "you better find the corpse first; I reckon that's a plenty for to-day. For all we know, there *ain't* any corpse and nobody hain't been murdered. That cuss could 'a' gone off somers and not been killed at all."

That graveled him and he says—

"Huck Finn, I never see such a person as you to want to spoil everything. As long as *you* can't see anything hopeful in a thing, you won't let anybody else. What good can it do you to throw cold water on that corpse and get up that selfish theory that there hain't been any murder? None in the world. I don't see how you can act so. I wouldn't treat you like that, and you know it. Here we've got a noble good opportunity to make a ruputation, and—"

"Oh, go ahead," I says, "I'm sorry and I take it all back. I didn't mean nothing. Fix it any way you want it. *He* ain't any consequence to me. If he's killed, I'm as glad of it as you are; and if he—"

"I never said anything about being glad; I only—"

"Well, then, I'm as *sorry* as you are. Any way you druther have it, that is the way *I* druther have it. He—"

"There ain't any druthers *about* it, Huck Finn; nobody said anything about druthers. And as for—"

He forgot he was talking, and went tramping along, studying. He begun to get excited again, and pretty soon he says—

"Huck, it'll be the bulliest thing that ever happened if we find the body after everybody else has quit looking, and then go ahead and hunt up the murderer. It won't only be an honor to us, but it 'll be an honor to uncle Silas because it was us that done it. It'll set him up again, you see if it don't."

But old Jeff Hooker he throwed cold water on the whole business when we got to his blacksmith shop and told him what we come for.

"You can take the dog," he says, "but you ain't a-going to find any corpse, because there ain't any corpse to find. Everybody's quit looking, and they're right. Soon as they come to think, they knowed there warn't no corpse. And I'll tell you for why. What does a person kill another person *for*, Tom Sawyer?—answer me that."

"Why, he—er—"

"Answer up! You ain't no fool. What does he kill him *for?*"

"Well, sometimes it's for revenge, and—"

"Wait. One thing at a time. Revenge, says you; and right you are. Now who ever had anything agin that poor trifling no-account? Who do you reckon would want to kill *him?*—that rabbit!"

Tom was stuck. I reckon he hadn't thought of a person having to have a reason for killing a person before, and now he see it warn't likely anybody would have that much of a grudge against a lamb like Jubiter Dunlap. The blacksmith says, by and by—

"The revenge idea won't work, you see. Well then, what's next? Robbery? B'gosh that must 'a' been it, Tom! Yes, sir-ree, I reckon we've struck it this time. Some feller wanted his gallus-buckles, and so he—"

But it was so funny he busted out laughing, and just went *on*

laughing and laughing and laughing till he was most dead, and Tom
looked so put out and cheap that I knowed he was ashamed he had
come, and wished he hadn't. But old Hooker never let up on him. He
raked up everything a person ever could want to kill another person
about; and any fool could see they didn't any of them fit this case, and
he just made no end of fun of the whole business and of the people that
had been hunting the body; and he said—

"If they'd had any sense they'd 'a' knowed the lazy cuss slid out
because he wanted a loafing spell after all this work. He'll come pot-
tering back in a couple of weeks, and then how'll you fellers feel? But
laws bless you, take the dog and go and hunt up his remainders. Do,
Tom."

Then he busted out and had another of them forty-rod laughs of
his'n. Tom couldn't back down after all this, so he said "All right,
unchain him," and the blacksmith done it and we started home and
left that old man laughing yet.

It was a lovely dog. There ain't any dog that's got a lovelier disposition than a bloodhound, and this one knowed us and liked us. He
capered and raced around, ever so friendly and powerful glad to be free
and have a holiday; but Tom was so cut up he couldn't take any
intrust in him and said he wished he'd stopped and thought a minute
before he ever started on such a fool errand. He said old Jeff Hooker
would tell everybody, and we'd never hear the last of it.

So we loafed along home down the back lanes, feeling pretty glum
and not talking. When we was passing the far corner of our tobacker
field we heard the dog set up a long howl in there, and we went to the
place and he was scratching the ground with all his might and every
now and then canting up his head sideways and fetching another
howl.

It was a long square the shape of a grave; the rain had made it sink
down and show the shape. The minute we come and stood there we
looked at one another and never said a word. When the dog had dug
down only a few inches he grabbed something and pulled it up and it
was an arm and a sleeve. Tom kind of gasped out and says—

"Come away, Huck—it's found."

I just felt awful. We struck for the road and fetched the first men
that come along. They got a spade at the crib and dug out the body, and

you never see such an excitement. You couldn't make anything out of
the face, but you didn't need to. Everybody said—

"Poor Jubiter; it's his clothes, to the last rag!"

Some rushed off to spread the news and tell the justice of the peace
and have an inquest, and me and Tom lit out for the house. Tom was
all afire and most out of breath when we come tearing in where uncle
Silas and aunt Sally and Benny was. Tom sung out—

"Me and Huck's found Jubiter Dunlap's corpse all by ourselves with
a bloodhound after everybody else had quit hunting and given it up;

"FETCHING ANOTHER HOWL."

and if it hadn't a been for us it never *would* 'a' been found; and he *was* murdered, too—they done it with a club or something like that; and I'm going to start in and find the murderer, next, and I bet I'll do it!"

Aunt Sally and Benny sprung up pale and astonished, but uncle Silas fell right forrard out of his chair onto the floor and groans out—

"Oh, my God, you've found him *now!*"

CHAPTER 10

THEM AWFUL WORDS froze us solid. We couldn't move hand or foot for as much as a half a minute. Then we kind of come to, and lifted the old man up and got him into his chair, and Benny petted him and kissed him and tried to comfort him, and poor old aunt Sally she done the same; but poor things they was so broke up and scared and knocked out of their right minds that they didn't hardly know what they was about. With Tom it was awful; it most petrified him to think maybe he had got his uncle into a thousand times more trouble than ever, and maybe it wouldn't ever happened if he hadn't been so ambitious to get celebrated, and let the corpse alone the way the others done. But pretty soon he sort of come to himself again and says—

"Uncle Silas, don't you say another word like that. It's dangerous, and there ain't a shadder of truth in it."

Aunt Sally and Benny was thankful to hear him say that, and they said the same; but the old man he wagged his head sorrowful and hopeless, and the tears run down his face and he says—

"No—I done it; poor Jubiter, I done it!"

It was dreadful to hear him say it. Then he went on and told about it; and said it happened the day me and Tom come—along about sundown. He said Jubiter pestered him and aggravated him till he was so mad he just sort of lost his mind and grabbed up a stick and hit him over the head with all his might, and Jubiter dropped in his tracks. Then he was scared and sorry, and got down on his knees and lifted his head up, and begged him to speak and say he wasn't dead; and before long he come to, and when he see who it was holding his head, he jumped like he was most scared to death, and cleared the fence and tore into the woods, and was gone. So he hoped he wasn't hurt bad.

"But laws," he says, "it was only just fear that give him that last little spurt of strength, and of course it soon played out and he laid down in the bush and there wasn't anybody to help him, and he died."

Then the old man cried and grieved, and said he was a murderer and

the mark of Cain was on him, and he had disgraced his family and was
going to be found out and hung. But Tom said—

"No, you ain't going to be found out. You *didn't* kill him. *One* lick
wouldn't kill him. Somebody else done it."

"Oh, yes," he says, "I done it—nobody else. Who else had anything
against him? Who else *could* have anything against him?"

He looked up kind of like he hoped some of us could mention
somebody that could have a grudge against that harmless no-account,
but of course it warn't no use—he *had* us; we couldn't say a word. He
noticed that, and he saddened down again and I never see a face so
miserable and so pitiful to see. Tom had a sudden idea and says—

"But hold on!—somebody *buried* him. Now who—"

He shut off sudden. I knowed the reason. It give me the cold shudders when he said them words, because right away I remembered
about us seeing uncle Silas prowling around with a long-handled
shovel away in the night that night. And I knowed Benny seen him,
too, because she was talking about it one day. The minute Tom shut
off he changed the subject and went to begging uncle Silas to keep
mum, and the rest of us done the same, and said he *must*, and said it
wasn't his business to tell on himself, and if he kept mum nobody
would ever know, but if it was found out and any harm come to him it
would break the family's hearts and kill them, and yet never do
anybody any good. So at last he promised. We was all of us more
comfortable, then, and went to work to cheer up the old man. We told
him all he'd got to do was to keep still and it wouldn't be long till the
whole thing would blow over and be forgot. We all said there wouldn't
anybody ever suspect uncle Silas, nor ever dream of such a thing, he
being so good and kind and having such a good character; and Tom
says, cordial and hearty, he says—

"Why, just look at it a minute; just consider. Here is uncle Silas, all
these years a preacher—at his own expense; all these years doing good
with all his might and every way he can think of—at his own expense,
all the time; always been loved by everybody, and respected; always
been peaceable and minding his own business, the very last man in
this whole deestrict to touch a person, and everybody knows it. Suspect *him*? Why, it ain't any more possible than—"

"By authority of the State of Arkansaw—I arrest you for the murder
of Jubiter Dunlap!" shouts the sheriff at the door.

It was awful. Aunt Sally and Benny flung themselves at uncle Silas,

screaming and crying, and hugged him and hung to him, and aunt
Sally said go away, she wouldn't ever give him up, they shouldn't have
him, and the niggers they come crowding and crying to the door
and—well, I couldn't stand it; it was enough to break a person's heart;
so I got out.

They took him up to the little one-horse jail in the village, and we all
went along to tell him good-bye, and Tom was feeling elegant, and says
to me, "We'll have a most noble good time and heaps of danger some
dark night, getting him out of there, Huck, and it'll be talked about
everywheres and we will be celebrated;" but the old man busted that
scheme up the minute he whispered to him about it. He said no, it was
his duty to stand whatever the law done to him, and he would stick to
the jail plum through to the end, even if there warn't no door to it. It
disappointed Tom, and graveled him a good deal, but he had to put up
with it.

But he felt responsible and bound to get his uncle Silas free; and he
told aunt Sally, the last thing, not to worry, because he was going to
turn in and work night and day and beat this game and fetch uncle
Silas out innocent; and she was very loving to him and thanked him
and said she knowed he would do his very best. And she told us to help
Benny take care of the house and the children, and then we had a
good-bye cry all around and went back to the farm, and left her there
to live with the jailer's wife a month till the trial in October.

CHAPTER 11

W<small>ELL, THAT WAS</small> a hard month on us all. Poor Benny, she kept up the best she could, and me and Tom tried to keep things cheerful there at the house, but it kind of went for nothing, as you may say. It was the same up at the jail. We went up every day to see the old people, but it was awful dreary, because the old man warn't sleeping much, and was walking in his sleep considerable, and so he got to looking fagged and miserable, and his mind got shaky, and we all got afraid his troubles would break him down and kill him. And whenever we tried to persuade him to feel cheerfuler, he only shook his head and said if we only knowed what it was to carry around a murderer's load on your heart we wouldn't talk that way. Tom and all of us kept telling him it *wasn't* murder, but just accidental killing, but it never made any difference—it was murder, and he wouldn't have it any other way. He actu'ly begun to come out plain and square towards trial-time and acknowledge that he *tried* to kill the man. Why, that was awful, you know. It made things seem fifty times as dreadful, and there warn't no more comfort for aunt Sally and Benny. But he promised he wouldn't say a word about his murder when others was around, and we was glad of that.

Tom Sawyer racked the head off of himself all that month trying to plan some way out for uncle Silas, and many's the night he kept me up most all night with this kind of tiresome work, but he couldn't seem to get on the right track no way. As for me, I reckoned a body might as well give it up, it all looked so blue and I was so down-hearted; but he wouldn't. He stuck to the business right along, and went on planning and thinking and ransacking his head.

So at last the trial come on, towards the middle of October, and we was all in the court. The place was jammed of course. Poor old uncle Silas, he looked more like a dead person than a live one, his eyes was so hollow and he looked so thin and so mournful. Benny she set on one

"KEPT ME UP MOST ALL NIGHT."

side of him and aunt Sally on the other, and they had veils on, and was full of trouble. But Tom he set by our lawyer, and had his finger in everywheres, of course. The lawyer let him, and the judge let him. He most took the business out of the lawyer's hands sometimes; which was well enough, because that was only a mud-turtle of a back-settlement lawyer and didn't know enough to come in when it rains, as the saying is.

They swore in the jury, and then the lawyer for the prostitution got up and begun. He made a terrible speech against the old man, that made him moan and groan, and made Benny and aunt Sally cry. The way *he* told about the murder kind of knocked us all stupid it was so different from the old man's tale. He said he was going to prove that uncle Silas was *seen* to kill Jubiter Dunlap by two good witnesses, and done it deliberate, and *said* he was going to kill him the very minute he hit him with the club; and they seen him hide Jubiter in the bushes, and they seen that Jubiter was stone-dead. And said uncle Silas come later and lugged Jubiter down into the tobacker field, and two men seen him do it. And said uncle Silas turned out, away in the night, and buried Jubiter, and a man seen him at it.

I says to myself, poor old uncle Silas has been lying about it because he reckoned nobody seen him and he couldn't bear to break aunt Sally's heart and Benny's; and right he was: as for me, I would 'a' lied the same way, and so would anybody that had any feeling, to save them such misery and sorrow which *they* warn't no ways responsible for. Well, it made our lawyer look pretty sick; and it knocked Tom

"OUR LAWYER."

silly, too, for a little spell, but then he braced up and let on that he warn't worried—but I knowed he *was*, all the same. And the people —my, but it made a stir amongst them!

And when that lawyer was done telling the jury what he was going to prove, he set down and begun to work his witnesses.

First, he called a lot of them to show that there was bad blood betwixt uncle Silas and the diseased; and they told how they had heard uncle Silas threaten the diseased, at one time and another, and how it got worse and worse and everybody was talking about it, and how diseased got afraid of his life, and told two or three of them he was certain uncle Silas would up and kill him some time or another.

Tom and our lawyer asked them some questions; but it warn't no use, they stuck to what they said.

Next, they called up Lem Beebe, and he took the stand. It come into my mind, then, how Lem and Jim Lane had come along talking, that time, about borrowing a dog or something from Jubiter Dunlap; and that brought up the blackberries and the lantern; and that brought up Bill and Jack Withers, and how *they* passed by, talking about a nigger stealing uncle Silas's corn; and that fetched up our old ghost that come along about the same time and scared us so—and here *he* was too, and a privileged character, on accounts of his being deef and dumb and a stranger, and they had fixed him a chair inside the railing, where he could cross his legs and be comfortable, whilst the other people was all in a jam so they couldn't hardly breathe. So it all come back to me just the way it was that day; and it made me mournful to think how pleasant it was up to then, and how miserable ever since.

Lem Beebe, sworn, said: "I was a-coming along, that day, second of September, and Jim Lane was with me, and it was towards sundown, and we heard loud talk, like quarreling, and we was very close, only the hazel bushes between (that's along the fence); and we heard a voice say, 'I've told you more'n once I'd kill you,' and knowed it was this prisoner's voice; and then we see a club come up above the bushes and down out of sight again, and heard a smashing thump and then a groan or two; and then we crope soft to where we could see, and there laid Jubiter Dunlap dead, and this prisoner standing over him with the club; and the next he hauled the dead man into a clump of bushes and hid him, and then we stooped low, to be out of sight, and got away."

Well, it was awful. It kind of froze everybody's blood to hear it, and the house was most as still whilst he was telling it as if there warn't nobody in it. And when he was done, you could hear them gasp and sigh, all over the house, and look at one another the same as to say, "Ain't it perfectly terrible—ain't it awful!"

Now happened a thing that astonished me. All the time the first witnesses was proving the bad blood and the threats and all that, Tom Sawyer was alive and laying for them; and the minute they was through, he went for them, and done his level best to catch them in lies and spile their testimony. But now, how different! When Lem first begun to talk, and never said anything about speaking to Jubiter or trying to borrow a dog off of him, he was all alive and laying for Lem, and you could see he was getting ready to cross-question him to death pretty soon, and then I judged him and me would go on the stand by and by and tell what we heard him and Jim Lane say. But the next time I looked at Tom I got the cold shivers. Why, he was in the brownest study you ever see—miles and miles away. He warn't hearing a word Lem Beebe was saying; and when he got through he was still in that brown study, just the same. Our lawyer joggled him, and then he looked up startled, and says, "Take the witness if you want him. Lemme alone—I want to think."

Well, that beat me. I couldn't understand it. And Benny and her mother—oh, they looked sick, they was so troubled. They shoved their veils to one side and tried to get his eye, but it warn't any use, and I couldn't get his eye either. So the mud-turtle he tackled the witness, but it didn't amount to nothing; and he made a mess of it.

Then they called up Jim Lane, and he told the very same story over again, exact. Tom never listened to this one at all, but set there thinking and thinking, miles and miles away. So the mud-turtle went in alone again and come out just as flat as he done before. The lawyer for the prostitution looked very comfortable, but the judge looked disgusted. You see, Tom was just the same as a regular lawyer, nearly, because it was Arkansaw law for a prisoner to choose anybody he wanted to help his lawyer, and Tom had had uncle Silas shove him into the case, and now he was botching it and you could see the judge didn't like it much.

All that the mud-turtle got out of Lem and Jim was this: he asked them—

"Why didn't you go and tell what you saw?"

"We was afraid we would get mixed up in it ourselves. And we was just starting down the river a-hunting for all the week besides; but as soon as we come back we found out they'd been searching for the body, so then we went and told Brace Dunlap all about it."

"When was that?"

"Saturday night, September 9th."

The judge he spoke up and says—

"Mr. Sheriff, arrest these two witnesses on suspicions of being accessionary after the fact to the murder."

The lawyer for the prostitution jumps up all excited, and says—

"Your Honor! I protest against this extraordi—"

"Set down!" says the judge, pulling his bowie and laying it on his pulpit. "I beg you to respect the Court."

So he done it. Then he called Bill Withers.

Bill Withers, sworn, said: "I was coming along about sundown, Saturday, September 2d, by the prisoner's field, and my brother Jack was with me, and we seen a man toting off something heavy on his back and allowed it was a nigger stealing corn; we couldn't see distinct; next we made out that it was one man carrying another; and the way it hung, so kind of limp, we judged it was somebody that was drunk; and by the man's walk we said it was parson Silas, and we judged he had found Sam Cooper drunk in the road, which he was always trying to reform him, and was toting him out of danger."

It made the people shiver to think of poor old uncle Silas toting off the diseased down to the place in his tobacker field where the dog dug up the body, but there warn't much sympathy around amongst the faces, and I heard one cuss say, "'Tis the coldest-blooded work I ever struck, lugging a murdered man around like that, and going to bury him like a animal, and him a preacher at that."

" 'SET DOWN!' SAYS THE JUDGE."

Tom he went on thinking, and never took no notice; so our lawyer took the witness and done the best he could, and it was plenty poor enough.

Then Jack Withers he come on the stand and told the same tale, just like Bill done.

And after him comes Brace Dunlap, and he was looking very mournful, and most crying; and there was a rustle and a stir all around, and everybody got ready to listen, and lots of the women folks said, "Poor cretur, poor cretur," and you could see a many of them wiping their eyes.

Brace Dunlap, sworn, said: "I was in considerable trouble a long time about my poor brother, but I reckoned things warn't near so bad as he made out, and I couldn't make myself believe anybody would have the heart to hurt a poor harmless cretur like that"—[by jings, I was sure I seen Tom give a kind of a faint little start, and then look disappointed again]—"and you know I *couldn't* think a preacher would hurt him—it warn't natural to think such an onlikely thing—so I never paid much attention, and now I sha'n't ever, ever forgive myself; for if I had a done different, my poor brother would be with me this day, and not laying yonder murdered, and him so harmless." He kind of broke down there and choked up, and waited to get his voice; and people all around said the most pitiful things, and women cried; and it was very still in there, and solemn, and old uncle Silas, poor thing, he give a groan right out so everybody heard him. Then Brace he went on, "Saturday, September 2d, he didn't come home to supper. By and by I got a little uneasy, and one of my niggers went over to this prisoner's place, but come back and said he warn't there. So I got uneasier and uneasier, and couldn't rest. I went to bed, but I couldn't sleep; and turned out, away late in the night, and went wandering over to this prisoner's place and all around about there a good while, hoping I would run across my poor brother, and never knowing he was out of his troubles and gone to a better shore—" So he broke down and choked up again, and most all the women was crying now. Pretty soon he got another start and says: "But it warn't no use; so at last I went home and tried to get some sleep, but couldn't. Well, in a day or two everybody was uneasy, and they got to talking about this prisoner's threats, and took to the idea, which I didn't take no stock in, that my brother was murdered; so they hunted around and tried to find his body, but couldn't and give it up. And so I reckoned he was gone off somers to have a little peace, and would come back to us when his troubles was kind of healed. But late Saturday night, the 9th, Lem Beebe and Jim Lane come to my house and told me all—told me the whole awful 'sassination, and my heart was broke. And *then* I remembered something that hadn't took no hold of me at the time, because reports said this prisoner had took to walking in his sleep and doing all kind of things of no consequence, not knowing what he was about. I will tell you what that thing was that come back into my memory. Away late that awful Saturday night when I was wandering around about this prisoner's place, grieving and troubled, I was down by the corner of the tobacker field and I heard a sound like digging in a gritty soil; and I crope nearer and peeped through the vines that hung on the rail fence and seen this prisoner *shoveling*—shoveling with a long-handled shovel—heaving earth into a big hole that was most filled up; his back was to me, but it was bright moonlight and I knowed him by his old green baize work-gown with a splattery white patch in the middle of the back like somebody had hit him with a snowball. *He was burying the man he'd murdered!*"

And he slumped down in his chair crying and sobbing, and most everybody in the house busted out wailing, and crying, and saying, "Oh, it's awful—awful—horrible!" and there was a most tremenduous excitement, and you couldn't hear yourself think; and right in the midst of it up jumps old uncle Silas, white as a sheet, and sings out—

"*It's true, every word—I murdered him in cold blood!*"

By Jackson, it petrified them! People rose up wild all over the house, straining and staring for a better look at him, and the judge was hammering with his mallet and the sheriff yelling "Order—order in the court—order!"

And all the while the old man stood there a-quaking and his eyes a-burning, and not looking at his wife and daughter, which was clinging to him and begging him to keep still, but pawing them off with his hands and saying he *would* clear his black soul from crime, he *would* heave off this load that was more than he could bear, and he *wouldn't* bear it another hour! And then he raged right along with his awful tale, everybody a-staring and gasping, judge, jury, lawyers, and everybody, and Benny and aunt Sally crying their hearts out. And by George, Tom Sawyer never looked at him once! Never once—just set there gazing with all his eyes at something else, I couldn't tell what. And so the old man raged right along, pouring his words out like a stream of fire:

"I killed him! I am guilty! But I never had the notion in my life to hurt him or harm him, spite of all them lies about my threatening him, till the very minute I raised the club—then my heart went cold!—then the pity all went out of it, and I struck to kill! In that one moment all my wrongs come into my mind; all the insults that that man and the scoundrel his brother, there, had put upon me, and how they had laid in together to ruin me with the people, and take away my good name, and *drive* me to some deed that would destroy me and my family that hadn't ever done *them* no harm, so help me God! And they done it in a mean revenge—for why? Because my innocent pure girl here at my side wouldn't marry that rich, insolent, ignorant coward, Brace Dunlap, who's been sniveling here over a brother he never cared a brass

"I STRUCK TO KILL!"

farthing for"—[I see Tom give a jump and look glad *this* time, to a dead certainty]—"and in that moment I've told you about, I forgot my God and remembered only my heart's bitterness—God forgive me! —and I struck to kill. In one second I was miserably sorry—oh, filled with remorse; but I thought of my poor family, and I *must* hide what I'd done for their sakes; and I did hide that corpse in the bushes; and presently I carried it to the tobacker field; and in the deep night I went with my shovel and buried it where—"

Up jumps Tom and shouts—

"*Now*, I've got it!" and waves his hand, oh, ever so fine and starchy, towards the old man, and says—

"Set down! A murder *was* done, but you never had no hand in it!"

"A MURDER *WAS* DONE."

Well, sir, you could a heard a pin drop. And the old man he sunk down kind of bewildered in his seat and aunt Sally and Benny didn't know it, because they was so astonished and staring at Tom with their mouths open and not knowing what they was about. And the whole house the same. *I* never seen people look so helpless and tangled up,

and I hain't ever seen eyes bug out and gaze without a blink the way
theirn did. Tom says, perfectly ca'm—

"Your Honor, may I speak?"

"For God's sake, yes—go on!" says the judge, so astonished and
mixed up he didn't know what he was about hardly.

Then Tom he stood there and waited a second or two—that was for
to work up an "effect," as he calls it—then he started in just as ca'm as
ever, and says:

"For about two weeks, now, there's been a little bill sticking on the
front of this court-house offering two thousand dollars reward for a
couple of big di'monds—stole at St. Louis. Them di'monds is worth
twelve thousand dollars. But never mind about that till I get to it. Now
about this murder. I will tell you all about it—how it happened—who
done it—every *de*tail."

You could see everybody nestle, now, and begin to listen for all they
was worth.

"This man here, Brace Dunlap, that's been sniveling so about his
dead brother that *you* know he never cared a straw for, wanted to
marry that young girl there, and she wouldn't have him. So he told
uncle Silas he would make him sorry. Uncle Silas knowed how
powerful he was, and how little chance he had against such a man, and
he was scared and worried, and done everything he could think of to
smooth him over and get him to be good to him: he even took his
no-account brother Jubiter on the farm and give him wages and stinted
his own family to pay them; and Jubiter done everything his brother
could contrive to insult uncle Silas, and fret and worry him, and try to
drive uncle Silas into doing him a hurt, so as to injure uncle Silas with
the people. And it done it. Everybody turned against him and said the
meanest kind of things about him, and it gradly broke his heart—yes,
and he was so worried and distressed that often he warn't hardly in his
right mind.

"Well, on that Saturday that we've had so much trouble about, two
of these witnesses here, Lem Beebe and Jim Lane, come along by where
uncle Silas and Jubiter Dunlap was at work—and that much of what
they've said is true, the rest is lies. They didn't hear uncle Silas say he
would kill Jubiter; they didn't hear no blow struck; they didn't see no
dead man, and they didn't see uncle Silas hide anything in the bushes.
Look at them now—how they set there, wishing they hadn't been so
handy with their tongues; anyway, they'll wish it before I get done.

"That same Saturday evening Bill and Jack Withers *did* see one man lugging off another one. That much of what they said is true, and the rest is lies. First off they thought it was a nigger stealing uncle Silas's corn—you notice it makes them look silly, now, to find out somebody overheard them say that. That's because they found out by and by who it was that was doing the lugging, and *they* know best why they swore here that they took it for uncle Silas by the gait—which it *wasn't*, and they knowed it when they swore to that lie.

"A man out in the moonlight *did* see a murdered person put under ground in the tobacker field—but it wasn't uncle Silas that done the burying. He was in his bed at that very time.

"Now, then, before I go on, I want to ask you if you've ever noticed this: that people, when they're thinking deep, or when they're worried, are most always doing something with their hands, and they don't know it, and don't notice what it is their hands are doing. Some stroke their chins; some stroke their noses; some stroke up *under* their chin with their hand; some twirl a chain, some fumble a button, then there's some that draws a figure or a letter with their finger on their cheek, or under their chin or on their under lip. That's *my* way. When I'm restless, or worried, or thinking hard, I draw capital V's on my cheek or on my under lip or under my chin, and never anything *but* capital V's—and half the time I don't notice it and don't know I'm doing it."

That was odd. That is just what I do; only I make an O. And I could see people nodding to one another, same as they do when they mean "*that's* so."

"Now then, I'll go on. That same Saturday—no, it was the night before—there was a steamboat laying at Flagler's Landing, forty miles above here, and it was raining and storming like the nation. And there was a thief aboard, and he had them two big di'monds that's advertised out here on this court-house door; and he slipped ashore with his hand-bag and struck out into the dark and the storm, and he was a-hoping he could get to this town all right and be safe. But he had two pals aboard the boat, hiding, and he knowed they was going to kill him the first chance they got and take the di'monds; because all three stole them, and then this fellow he got hold of them and skipped.

"Well, he hadn't been gone more'n ten minutes before his pals found it out, and they jumped ashore and lit out after him. Prob'ly they burnt matches and found his tracks. Anyway, they dogged along

after him all day Saturday and kept out of his sight; and towards
sundown he come to the bunch of sycamores down by uncle Silas's
field, and he went in there to get a disguise out of his hand-bag and put
it on before he showed himself here in the town—and mind you he
done that just a little after the time that uncle Silas was hitting Jubiter
Dunlap over the head with a club—for he *did* hit him.

"But the minute the pals see that thief slide into the bunch of
sycamores, they jumped out of the bushes and slid in after him.

"They fell on him and clubbed him to death.

"Yes, for all he screamed and howled so, they never had no mercy on
him, but clubbed him to death. And two men that was running along
the road heard him yelling that way, and they made a rush into the
sycamore bunch—which was where they was bound for, anyway
—and when the pals saw them they lit out and the two new men after
them a-chasing them as tight as they could go. But only a minute or
two—then these two new men slipped back very quiet into the sycamores.

"*Then* what did they do? I will tell you what they done. They found
where the thief had got his disguise out of his carpet-sack to put on; so
one of them strips and puts on that disguise."

Tom waited a little here, for some more "effect"—then he says, very
deliberate—

"The man that put on that dead man's disguise was—*Jubiter Dunlap!*"

"Great Scott!" everybody shouted, all over the house, and old uncle
Silas he looked perfectly astonished.

"Yes, it was Jubiter Dunlap. Not dead, you see. Then they pulled off
the dead man's boots and put Jubiter Dunlap's old ragged shoes on the
corpse and put the corpse's boots on Jubiter Dunlap. Then Jubiter
Dunlap stayed where he was, and the other man lugged the dead body
off in the twilight; and after midnight he went to uncle Silas's house,
and took his old green work-robe off of the peg where it always hangs
in the passage betwixt the house and the kitchen and put it on, and
stole the long-handled shovel and went off down into the tobacker
field and buried the murdered man."

He stopped, and stood a half a minute. Then—

"And who do you reckon the murdered man *was*? It was—*Jake*
Dunlap, the long-lost burglar!"

"Great Scott!"

"And the man that buried him was—*Brace* Dunlap, his brother!"

"Great Scott!"

"And who do you reckon is this mowing idiot here that's letting on all these weeks to be a deef and dumb stranger? It's—*Jubiter* Dunlap!"

My land, they all busted out in a howl, and you never see the like of that excitement since the day you was born. And Tom he made a jump for Jubiter and snaked off his goggles and his false whiskers, and there was the murdered man, sure enough, just as alive as anybody! And aunt Sally and Benny they went to hugging and crying and kissing and smothering old uncle Silas to that degree he was more muddled and confused and mushed up in his mind than he ever was before, and that is saying considerable. And next, people begun to yell—

"Tom Sawyer! Tom Sawyer! Shut up everybody, and let him go on! Go on, Tom Sawyer!"

"AND THERE WAS THE MURDERED MAN."

"WHICH MADE HIM FEEL UNCOMMON BULLY."

Which made him feel uncommon bully, for it was nuts for Tom Sawyer to be a public character thataway, and a hero, as he calls it. So when it was all quiet, he says—

"There ain't much left, only this. When that man there, Brace Dunlap, had most worried the life and sense out of uncle Silas till at last he plum lost his mind and hit this other blatherskite his brother with a club, I reckon he seen his chance. Jubiter broke for the woods to hide, and I reckon the game was for him to slide out, in the night, and leave the country. Then Brace would make everybody believe uncle Silas killed him and hid his body somers; and that would ruin uncle Silas and drive *him* out of the country—hang him, maybe; I dunno. But when they found their dead brother in the sycamores without knowing him, because he was so battered up, they see they had a better thing; disguise *both* and bury Jake and dig him up presently all dressed up in Jubiter's clothes, and hire Jim Lane and Bill Withers and the others to swear to some handy lies—which they done. And there they set, now, and I told them they would be looking sick before I got done, and that is the way they're looking now.

"Well, me and Huck Finn here, we come down on the boat with the thieves, and the dead one told us all about the di'monds, and said the others would murder him if they got the chance; and we was going to help him all we could. We was bound for the sycamores when we heard them killing him in there; but we was in there in the early morning after the storm and allowed nobody hadn't been killed, after all. And when we see Jubiter Dunlap here spreading around in the very same disguise Jake told us *he* was going to wear, we thought it was Jake his own self—and he was goo-gooing deef and dumb, and *that* was according to agreement.

"Well, me and Huck went on hunting for the corpse after the others quit, and we found it. And was proud, too; but uncle Silas he knocked us crazy by telling us *he* killed the man. So we was mighty sorry we found the body, and was bound to save uncle Silas's neck if we could; and it was going to be tough work, too, because he wouldn't let us break him out of prison the way we done with our old nigger Jim, you remember.

"I done everything I could the whole month to think up some way to save uncle Silas, but I couldn't strike a thing. So when we come into court to-day I come empty, and couldn't see no chance anywheres. But by and by I had a glimpse of something that set me thinking—just a little wee glimpse—only that, and not enough to make sure; but it set me thinking hard—and *watching*, when I was only letting on to think; and by and by, sure enough, when uncle Silas was piling out that stuff about *him* killing Jubiter Dunlap, I catched that glimpse again, and this time I jumped up and shut down the proceedings, because I *knowed* Jubiter Dunlap was a-setting here before me. I knowed him by a thing which I seen him do—and I remembered it. I'd seen him do it when I was here a year ago."

He stopped then, and studied a minute—laying for an "effect"—I knowed it perfectly well. Then he turned off like he was going to leave the platform, and says, kind of lazy and indifferent—

"Well, I believe that is all."

Why, you never heard such a howl!—and it come from the whole house:

"What *was* it you seen him do? Stay where you are, you little devil! You think you are going to work a body up till his mouth's a-watering and stop there? What *was* it he done?"

That was it, you see—he just done it to get an "effect;" you couldn't 'a' pulled him off of that platform with a yoke of oxen.

"Oh, it wasn't anything much," he says. "I seen him looking a little excited when he found uncle Silas was actuly fixing to hang himself for a murder that warn't ever done; and he got more and more nervous and worried, I a-watching him sharp but not seeming to look at him —and all of a sudden his hands begun to work and fidget, and pretty soon his left crept up and *his finger drawed a cross on his cheek*, and then I *had* him!"

Well, then they ripped and howled and stomped and clapped their hands till Tom Sawyer was that proud and happy he didn't know what to do with himself. And then the judge he looked down over his pulpit and says—

"My boy, did you *see* all the various details of this strange conspiracy and tragedy that you've been describing?"

"No, your Honor, I didn't see any of them."

"Didn't see any of them! Why, you've told the whole history straight through, just the same as if you'd seen it with your eyes. How did you manage that?"

Tom says, kind of easy and comfortable—

"Oh, just noticing the evidence and piecing this and that together, your Honor; just an ordinary little bit of detective work; anybody could 'a' done it."

"Nothing of the kind! Not two in a million could 'a' done it. You are a very remarkable boy."

Then they let go and give Tom another smashing round, and he— well, he wouldn't 'a' sold out for a silver mine. Then the judge says—

"But are you certain you've got this curious history straight?"

"Perfectly, your Honor. Here is Brace Dunlap—let him deny his share of it if he wants to take the chance; I'll engage to make him wish he hadn't said anything. . . . Well, you see *he's* pretty quiet. And his brother's pretty quiet, and them four witnesses that lied so and got paid for it, they're pretty quiet. And as for uncle Silas, it ain't any use for him to put in his oar, I wouldn't believe him under oath!"

Well, sir, that fairly made them shout; and even the judge he let go and laughed. Tom he was just feeling like a rainbow. When they was done laughing he looks up at the judge and says—

"Your Honor, there's a thief in this house."

"A thief?"

"Yes, sir. And he's got them twelve-thousand-dollar di'monds on him."

By gracious, but it made a stir! Everybody went to shouting—

"Which is him? which is him? p'int him out!"

And the judge says—

"Point him out, my lad. Sheriff, you will arrest him. Which one is it?"

Tom says—

"This late dead man here—Jubiter Dunlap."

Then there was another thundering let-go of astonishment and excitement; but Jubiter, which was astonished enough before, was just fairly putrefied with astonishment this time. And he spoke up, about half crying, and says—

"Now *that's* a lie! Your Honor, it ain't fair; I'm plenty bad enough without that. I done the other things—Brace he put me up to it, and persuaded me, and promised he'd make me rich, some day, and I done it, and I'm sorry I done it, and I wisht I hadn't; but I hain't stole no di'monds, and I hain't got no di'monds; I wisht I may never stir if it ain't so. The sheriff can search me and see."

Tom says—

"Your Honor, it wasn't right to call him a thief, and I'll let up on that a little. He did steal the di'monds, but he didn't know it. He stole them from his brother Jake when he was laying dead, after Jake had stole them from the other thieves; but Jubiter didn't know he was stealing them; and he's been swelling around here with them a month; yes, sir, twelve thousand dollars' worth of di'monds on him—all that riches, and going around here every day just like a poor man. Yes, your Honor, he's got them on him now."

The judge spoke up and says—

"Search him, sheriff."

Well, sir, the sheriff he ransacked him high and low, and everywhere: searched his hat, socks, seams, boots, everything—and Tom he stood there quiet, laying for another of them effects of his'n. Finally the sheriff he give it up, and everybody looked disappointed, and Jubiter says—

"There, now! what'd I tell you?"

And the judge says—

"It appears you were mistaken this time, my boy."

Then Tom he took an attitude and let on to be studying with all his might, and scratching his head. Then all of a sudden he glanced up chipper, and says—

"Oh, now I've got it! I'd forgot."

Which was a lie, and I knowed it. Then he says—

"Will somebody be good enough to lend me a little small screw-driver? There was one in your brother's hand-bag that you smouched, Jubiter, but I reckon you didn't fetch it with you."

"No, I didn't. I didn't want it, and I give it away."

"That was because you didn't know what it was for."

Jubiter had his boots on again, by now, and when the thing Tom wanted was passed over the people's heads till it got to him, he says to Jubiter—

"Put up your foot on this chair." And he kneeled down and begun to unscrew the heel-plate, everybody watching; and when he got that big di'mond out of that boot-heel and held it up and let it flash and blaze and squirt sunlight everwhichaway, it just took everybody's breath; and Jubiter he looked so sick and sorry you never see the like of it. And when Tom held up the other di'mond he looked sorrier than ever. Land! he was thinking how he would 'a' skipped out and been rich and independent in a foreign land if he'd only had the luck to guess what the screw-driver was in the carpet-bag for.

Well, it was a most exciting time, take it all around, and Tom got cords of glory. The judge took the di'monds, and stood up in his pulpit, and cleared his throat, and shoved his spectacles back on his head, and says—

"I'll keep them and notify the owners; and when they send for them it will be a real pleasure to me to hand you the two thousand dollars, for you've earned the money—yes, and you've earned the deepest and most sincerest thanks of this community besides, for lifting a wronged and innocent family out of ruin and shame, and saving a good and honorable man from a felon's death, and for exposing to infamy and the punishment of the law a cruel and odious scoundrel and his miserable creatures!"

Well, sir, if there'd been a brass band to bust out some music, then, it would 'a' been just the perfectest thing I ever see, and Tom Sawyer he said the same.

Then the sheriff he nabbed Brace Dunlap and his crowd, and by and by next month the judge had them up for trial and jailed the whole lot. And everybody crowded back to uncle Silas's little old church, and was ever so loving and kind to him and the family and couldn't do enough for them; and uncle Silas he preached them the blamedest jumbledest idiotic sermons you ever struck, and would tangle you up so you couldn't find your way home in daylight; but the people never let on but what they thought it was the clearest and brightest and elegantest sermons that ever was; and they would set there and cry, for love and pity; but, by George, they give me the jim-jams and the fan-tods and caked up what brains I had, and turned them solid; but by and by they loved the old man's intellects back into him again and he was as sound in his skull as ever he was, which ain't no flattery, I reckon. And so the whole family was as happy as birds, and nobody could be gratefuler and lovinger than what they was to Tom Sawyer; and the same to me, though I hadn't done nothing. And when the two thousand dollars come, Tom give half of it to me, and never told anybody so, which didn't surprise me, because I knowed him.

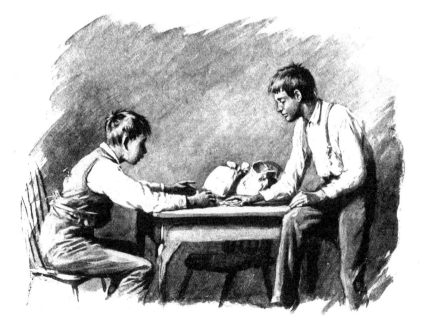

"TOM GIVE HALF OF IT TO ME."

EXPLANATORY NOTES

Notes are keyed to page and line: 1.4 means page 1, line 4. Chapter titles and picture captions are not included when counting lines. Some of the notes included here are based on notes first published in the full California scholarly edition, described in the Note on the Texts (p. 188).

TOM SAWYER ABROAD

xiv.2   Jean Clemens] Mark Twain's youngest daughter, who was fourteen when the American edition of *Tom Sawyer Abroad* was published. The author wrote this dedication to her, but failed to give it to his publisher in time; it is included here because he instructed his publisher to include it in the second edition.

1.1-2   all them adventures] Those recounted by Huck in *Adventures of Huckleberry Finn.*

1.4   pisoned him for more] Perversely increased his desire for more.

1.13   laid over] Surpassed; was regarded as superior to.

2.3   mortal] Mortally: extremely; excessively.

2.3   reckoned] Considered; thought; supposed; calculated.

2.7   jim-jams] Fidgets; creeps; fit of depression.

2.22   dry gripes] Strong repugnance. Literally, pain in the bowels.

2.24   ten cents] From 1816 until 1845, postage was ten cents on a letter consisting of one piece of paper not going over 80 miles; from 1846 until 1851 the same rate applied to any letter not going over 300 miles. In 1851, the limit was extended to 3,000 miles.

3.13   four cities] Nat Parsons would undoubtedly have gone to St. Louis by boat, and then by stagecoach or horseback to

Vandalia, Illinois, where he would have taken the Cumberland Road, or National Road as it was also called, for Washington, thus passing through St. Louis, Columbus, Wheeling, and Baltimore.

3.17   bottoms] Low-lying lands, usually along a river.

4.1   shoved out] Decamped; departed; set out for.

4.31-32 tuckered out] Exhausted.

5.8   eclipse] There were solar eclipses observable in the United States on 28 July 1842 and 8 July 1851. An eclipse would start a revival because of the widespread superstition that it was a portent of disaster—even the end of the world.

5.28   git come up with] Are gotten the better of.

6.12   cam] Calm.

6.13   paynim] Pagans (Mohammedans).

7.32   Richard Cur de Lyon] Richard Coeur de Lion, or Richard I (1157–1199), won great fame in the Third Crusade, 1191–1192.

7.32   Godfrey de Bulloyn] Godfrey de Bouillon was elected ruler in Jerusalem in 1099.

7.37   yahoos] Bumpkins; greenhorns.

8.20   Sny] A narrow passage in the Mississippi River between the Illinois shore and an island opposite Hannibal, Missouri.

8.35   sutler] A tradesman who sells provisions to an army.

9.4   allowed] Concluded; thought or believed; declared; maintained.

9.6   Walter Scott's books] One of these was undoubtedly *The Talisman.*

9.10   shook] Left behind; got rid of.

10.4   balloon that was going to sail to Europe] Mark Twain may have been thinking of a balloon owned by John Wise which left St. Louis for Europe on 1 July 1859, but got only as far as New York. Mark Twain had been interested in flying machines at least since 1869, when Frederick Marriott's "Avitor"—a cigar-shaped balloon equipped with fixed wings and two propellers—achieved flight in San Francisco. "It is a subject that is bound to stir the pulses of any man," he wrote his newspaper, "for in this age of inventive wonders all men have come to believe that in some genius' brain sleeps the solution of the grand problem of aerial navigation—and along with that belief is the hope that that genius will reveal his miracle before they die, and likewise a dread that he will poke off somewhere and die himself before he finds out that he has such a wonder lying dormant in his brain. We all *know* the air can be navigated—therefore, hurry up your sails and bladders— satisfy us—let us have peace."

13.8   graveled him] Irritated, provoked him; went against his grain.

14.1   pepper-box revolver] An early revolver having five or six barrels that revolved on a central axis. Also called a "coffee-mill."

16.20   rusty] Tired, sleepy; inclined to stretch.

18.14   muggins] Fool; simpleton.

19.26   blatherskites] Those who talk blatant nonsense; bluster- ing, talkative persons.

19.37   chuckleheads] Dense or stupid persons.

20.13   silver turnip] An old-fashioned thick watch with a silver case.

22.25   putrified] Petrified.

24.5   Plum] Plumb: exactly.

24.15-16 sextant] An instrument for measuring the altitudes of celestial bodies in order to determine latitude and lon- gitude.

25.5   whet] Small drink of liquor.

27.10   gunnel] Gunwale, the top edge of the side of the "boat" under the balloon.

29.18   we druther] We'd rather.

31.7   *Welkin*] A fancy, literary term for sky, or heavens. As Tom says later in the chapter, "it just meant out-doors and up high" (33.2-3).

31.8   red wafer] Sealing wax.

31.10   *Erronort*] Tom's spelling of "aeronaut." As he says later, aeronauts were persons who "sailed around in balloons" (33.9).

32.6   bricked us up] Gave us pause; reduced us to silence. Literally, closed us up with brickwork.

32.24   ornithologers] Ornithologists (those who study birds). In the nineteenth century it was standard scientific practice to kill birds for study.

35.4   gashly] Ghastly.

35.5   rounds] Rungs.

37.24   originals] Forebears.

38.2   Grinnage time] Greenwich time. The time of Greenwich, England, is used as the standard of reference throughout the world.

38.34   lunkhead] Thick-headed or slow-witted person.

41.24   yahoo] Here apparently in the English sense of brute or uncouth character.

41.37   snake] Snatch or carry quickly.

45.16   Eyetalian] Italian.

46.10   biled] Boiled.

48.36   Sam Hill] Euphemism for "hell."

49.22   tale about a camel driver] "The Anecdote of an Impudent Camel Driver" in *The Arabian Nights.*

51.4   duffers] Persons without practical abilities; incompetents; stupid or foolish persons.

51.10-11 like the nation] Euphemism for "like damnation."

52.2   bammy] Balmy.

55.18   *my*ridge] Mirage.

56.5   Anna Nias en Suffira] Both Ananias and Sapphira, his wife, fell down and died when accused by Peter of lying (Acts 5:1-11).

56.28   passel] Parcel. Used contemptuously to mean a lot, quantity, or pack.

56.37   orneriest] Worst; poorest in quality; most commonplace or ordinary.

57.23	phaze] Faze: discompose or disturb.
57.27	harum-scarum] Recklessly, wildly.
58.9	bells letters] Belles lettres: fine literature.
58.12	polly-voo] Parlez-vous: speak French.
58.37	sk'yers] Scares.
59.1	'clah] I declare.
59.24-25	Let her go to starboard!—port your hellum!] Tom is confused about his nautical terms. "To starboard" means to the right; "port your helm" means turn left.
60.26	boxing-mill] Undisciplined circling and punching as distinct from scientific boxing or serious fighting.
61.7	camp meeting] Religious meeting held in the open air or under a tent; usually a revival.
62.9	jack-legged] Lacking professional training or skill; makeshift.
63.3	cans] Tin cans first began to replace glass containers in the United States in 1839.
63.8	too gay] Literally too fine, too good. Huck means that the beef has ripened to the point where it seems spoiled.
63.26	pam] Palm.
64.30	roach-backed] Having an upward-curving back.
64.31	whole biling] Entire lot.
65.31	two or three years ago] Mexico surrendered its claim to California in the treaty of Guadalupe Hidalgo in 1848. Tom's statement implies that the date of his balloon trip was about 1850 or 1851.
67.27	sockdologer] Tremendous, decisive blow.
67.32	lifter] Heavy blow. Figuratively, enough to lift someone off his feet.
68.11	dickens's own time] Euphemism for "devil's own time," an extremely difficult time.
68.16	bluest] Most morally strict; gravest. A "blue-skin" was a nickname applied to Presbyterians because of their allegedly grave deportment.
68.23	dervish] Moslem monk or friar.

68.25-26   out of the Arabian Nights] "The Story of the Blind Baba-Abdalla" in *The Arabian Nights.*

69.4   ornery] Cantankerous; irritable.

69.6   ams] Alms.

72.11   beat] Deadbeat: a worthless person; a loafer or idler who sponges on his friends.

73.20   loddanum] Laudanum: tincture of opium.

74.16   truck] Stuff.

75.10   Captain Kidd] A Scottish navigator (?1645–1701) who was feared as a pirate and notorious for having buried his vast treasures.

76.6   a rattler] Extraordinary.

76.13   nobby] Extremely smart or elegant.

78.31   handle] Title.

78.36   simmeters] Scimitars: curved swords or sabers.

80.2   diseased] Deceased.

82.29   Creesus] Croesus, king of ancient Lydia in Asia Minor during the sixth century B.C. His enormous wealth was proverbial.

83.2   bust] Break financially; bankrupt.

83.5-6   bluer and bluer] Gloomier and gloomier.

84.27   come-off] Excuse.

85.6   got shut of it] Got rid of it.

88.1   Methusalem] Methuselah, reported in Genesis 5:27 to have lived to the age of 969.

89.2   Noureddin, and Bedreddin] Noureddin was the hero of "Noureddin and the Fair Princess" in *The Arabian Nights;* he was not a giant. Bedreddin is not a character but a pun on "bedridden."

90.11-12   they had just lately dug the sand away and found that little temple] In 1852–1853 a group under the direction of A. Mariette, the French Egyptologist, cleared the accumulated sand away from the Sphinx and discovered an ancient granite and alabaster sanctuary now variously called the Granite Temple and the Valley Building of Chephren.

91.8   a-biling] Rapidly and perhaps fiercely.

93.19   Bronze Horse] In the story entitled "The Magic Horse"
            in *The Arabian Nights* the Prince of Persia rescues the
            Princess of El-Yemen on an ebony and ivory horse. At
            no time, however, do they alight on a pyramid, nor are
            they even in Egypt.

95.21   chirk up] Cheer up; become lively or attentive.

98.7   Koran] The sacred book of the Mohammedans.

98.11   ain't a circumstance] Nothing in comparison with.

98.17   sugar-loaf] Conical.

98.37-38   house where . . . and the new ones] "The Story of Ali
            Cogia" in *The Arabian Nights*. A cadi was a civil judge.

100.16   mershum] Meerschaum: a pipe with a bowl of very light,
            porous clay.

100.37   bulge] Rush, dash.

101   *illustration*] Mark Twain provided a sketch of this map
            in his manuscript. The map was redrawn, with added de-
            tails, by the illustrator Daniel Beard.

102.3   tell-tale] A gauge, here used to indicate wind velocity.

102.11   pison] Extremely; excessively.

102.29   slouch] Slouch hat, one with a broad and drooping brim.
            The illustrator of the book portrayed all of the travelers
            with top hats.

103.2   *where the Ark was*] Noah's ark came to rest on Mount
            Ararat, not Mount Sinai.

TOM SAWYER, DETECTIVE

107.1   next spring] As at the beginning of *Tom Sawyer Abroad*,
            Huck refers to events recorded in his *Adventures of
            Huckleberry Finn*, not in *The Adventures of Tom Sawyer*.

108.10   trapsing] Walking idly or without specific purpose;
            tramping.

110.10   pine blank] Point blank: directly; flatly.

110.18   a whole grist] A great number.

110.27   ornery] Poor in quality; worthless or no-account; com-
            monplace or ordinary.

110.35   Jubiter and his moons] In the 1840s only the four moons discovered by Galileo were known. A fifth was discovered in 1892, which Mark Twain may have known. Jupiter is now known to have at least thirteen moons.

111.30   chuckle-headed] Stupid or dense.

111.32   reckon] Think; suppose.

112.2   sternwheeler] A steamboat propelled by a paddlewheel at the stern, or rear.

112.3   one-horse] Petty; contemptibly small; insignificant.

112.4-5   Upper Mississippi . . . Lower Mississippi] The "upper river" extended from the confluence with the Missouri River northward to St. Paul; the "lower river" from the confluence southward to New Orleans.

112.13   allowed] Concluded; thought or believed; declared; maintained.

112.23   mischief] Euphemism for "devil."

112.25   nuts] A source of pleasure or delight.

113.3   Elexandria, up on the Iowa line] Alexandria, Missouri, on the border with Iowa.

113.16   apern] Apron.

113.29   truck] Stuff; miscellaneous articles of little value; here, odds and ends of food and utensils.

114.5-6   spit'n image] Spit and image: the very likeness or image.

114.22   shook him] Rejected him; turned her back on him.

114.32   The nation] Euphemism for "damnation."

115.11   blue goggles] Glasses with blue lenses.

118.19-20   another mangy rough deck passenger] For every cabin passenger living in the relative elegance of the upper deck on a typical Mississippi riverboat there would be as many as four or five deck passengers crowded together below with no bed, no food other than what they brought aboard, no toilet facilities, often not even enough deck space on which to lie down. Deck passengers were not allowed on the upper deck except, as in the case of the boat described here, to buy drinks at a carefully designated bar.

118.25   boots] Servant who cleaned and polished boots and shoes.

120.16-17   second-hand slop-shop] Store where used ready-made clothes were sold.

120.21   rusty] Shabby; unkempt; uncouth.

121.2   guard] The part of a steamboat's deck that extended beyond the hull, built especially on the sidewheel type of steamboat so as to curve out over and protect the paddle-wheels. A distinctive feature of all western steamboats, whether sidewheel or sternwheel.

121.5-6   hurricane deck] Upper deck.

121.6   plum] Plumb: completely.

122.2   showed the white feather] Showed himself a coward. An allusion to the belief that a white feather in a game-bird's tail was a sign of inferior breeding, making it unsuitable for fighting.

122.22   *do* for him] Kill him; do him in.

123.3   bully] First-rate; excellent; splendid.

123.14   blatherskite] One who talks blatant nonsense; blustering, talkative person.

123.16   pudd'nheads] Fools.

124.6   deal table] One made from a board of pine or fir, about eleven inches wide by two-and-a-half thick.

126.19   plum] Plumb: exactly.

127.22   torch-basket] A fixture for holding torches for illumination on a steamboat.

127.30   tight] Rapidly; quickly.

132.2   stile] Step or set of steps for passing over a fence.

132.2-3   where old Jim's cabin was . . . the time we set him free] Huck refers to the concluding chapters of *Huckleberry Finn*.

132.11   smouched] Taken; pilfered.

132.16   scollop the facts] Scallop: embroider; embellish the facts.

134.34   baize] Coarse woolen cloth with a nap on one side.

135.6   traps] Trappings; baggage; belongings.

136.18-19   as straight as a string] Like a string on a fiddle.

136.26   lay] Wager; bet.

136.35   allowed] Intended.

137.2   tuckered out] Exhausted.

140.15   shin out] Use one's legs; move around quickly.

145.5   give me the fan-tods] Made me nervous, fidgety, uneasy.

148.1   bullyrag] Badger; harass.

149.3   rattling] Extraordinary.

149.5-6   hog and hominy] Pork and corn.

149.10   admired to hear] Liked or wanted to hear.

151.7   you druther] You'd rather.

151.9   druthers] Choice; preference.

151.37   gallus-buckles] Suspender-buttons.

152.9-10   pottering] Sauntering; dawdling.

152.11   remainders] Remains; corpse.

152.13   forty-rod] Violent; prodigious. Derived from "forty-rod whisky," strong whisky facetiously warranted to kill a man at that distance.

152.37   crib] Corn crib: a bin for storing corn.

157.14   graveled him] Went against his grain; irritated, provoked him.

159.8   prostitution] Prosecution.

160.15   diseased] Deceased.

163.1   bowie] Bowie knife; see the illustration.

167.10   starchy] Grandly; impressively; elegantly.

171.4   mowing] Grimacing.

171.8   snaked] Snatched.

173.19   the way we done with our old nigger Jim] Described in the final chapters of *Huckleberry Finn*.

175.15   putrefied] Petrified.

176.26   cords] A large quantity. The analogy is to cords of wood, stacks eight feet by four by four.

177.10   jim-jams] Fidgets; creeps; fit of depression.

NOTE ON THE TEXTS

The texts of Mark Twain's two stories published here are, for the most part, photographic reproductions of the texts published in 1980 by the University of California Press in volume 4 of the Works of Mark Twain: *The Adventures of Tom Sawyer; Tom Sawyer Abroad; and Tom Sawyer, Detective,* edited by John C. Gerber, Paul Baender, and Terry Firkins. Mr. Firkins, under the direction of Mr. Baender at the University of Iowa, established both texts from the available documents and secured the approval of the Center for Editions of American Authors (CEAA). Editorial work on the original edition was supported by grants from the United States Office of Education and from the Research Materials Program of the National Endowment for the Humanities (NEH). For this Mark Twain Library edition the 1980 texts have been partly reset to correct minor errors (listed at the end of this note) and to accommodate the original illustrations. The Mark Twain Project staff carried out these changes: Victor Fischer and Harriet Elinor Smith redesigned the pages to incorporate the illustrations and, with Richard E. Bucci, Janet E. Leigh, and me, checked all reset and new matter in accord with the proofreading standards of the CEAA. David J. Nordloh, chairman of the Committee on Scholarly Editions, granted permission to use the CEAA seal, contingent on this process of verification.

TOM SAWYER ABROAD

Mr. Firkins established the text of this story from four authoritative documents: (1) Mark Twain's manuscript in the Henry W. and Albert A. Berg Collection of The New York Public Library; (2) the first American typesetting, consisting of six installments in *St. Nicholas* magazine (November 1893–April 1894); (3) the first English edition, published by Chatto & Windus on 14 April 1894; and (4) the first American edition, published by Charles L. Webster and Co. on 16 April 1894. The following account is based on Mr. Firkins' introduction and notes, supplemented by documents in the Mark Twain Papers at Berkeley.

Mark Twain wrote his story rapidly in August 1892, while living in Germany. He ordered a typescript, with at least one carbon copy, made from the manuscript. He then revised these typescripts before sending one of them (in two installments, on 14 September and 11 October 1892) to Frederick J. Hall, his New York publisher, while retaining the carbon copy with most of his revisions copied onto it for safekeeping. In mid-November 1892, Mary Mapes Dodge, editor-in-chief of the children's magazine *St. Nicholas*, told Mark Twain she would pay him $4,000 for the story and would publish it in the fall of 1893. On 2 December 1892 Mark Twain agreed to these terms, and Hall provided her with the revised typescript from which both the typesetter and the illustrator, Daniel Carter Beard, would work. Mark Twain was aware that his story might be censored on behalf of the magazine's young audience, for on 31 October he had written to Hall: "I tried to leave the improprieties all out; if I didn't, Mrs. Dodge can scissor them out."

Mark Twain inspected the illustrations before the first installment appeared in mid-October, and he also read some of the text in proof. On 26 September he reported having visited the *St. Nicholas* offices with his former servant George Griffin, who was black, and whose easy familiarity with Mark Twain "seemed to puzzle [the editors] a good deal. I showed him a number of engravings (artist's proofs) for 'Tom Sawyer Abroad' & asked for his opinion of them—& that puzzled those editors again." Probably on 17 October, just after the first installment had appeared, Mark Twain reported a less tranquil visit: "I have been to St. Nicholas to curse the proof-reader's attempts to improve my spelling and punctuation. He had also written some suggestions in the margin. But Clarke [the associate editor] will have the matter set according to copy hereafter and see that the proof-reader retains his suggestions in the mush of his decayed brain." In 1939, Dan Beard recalled that at least some of Mark Twain's anger was directed at Mrs. Dodge instead of the proofreader:

> When Mark read the proof he was exceedingly wroth and, entering the sanctum sanctorum, the holy of holies, or the editorial department of *St Nicholas*, he shocked the gentle creatures and terrified the associate editors by exclaiming, "Any editor to whom I submit

my manuscripts has an undisputed right to delete anything to which he objects but"—and his brows knit as he cried—"God Almighty Himself has no right to put words in my mouth that I never used!" After smelling salts were administered to the whole editorial staff, and the editor in chief was resuscitated, the mistake was remedied, the error rectified, and things went smoothly.

Although the editor's suggestions were not incorporated, her extensive deletions and substitutions were followed. Indecorous references to death, perspiration, profanity, and religion—including Tom's explanation of how medieval popes developed the art of swearing (chapter 8) —were modified or completely omitted. As Dan Beard also recalled, this squeamishness extended even to the drawings he had provided. "My illustrations of Huck Finn, Tom Sawyer and Nigger Jim [were] returned to me, the editor ruling that it was excessively coarse and vulgar to depict them with *bare feet!* I was asked to cover their nakedness with shoes." Beard complied, "mentally asking" the characters' "forgiveness" as he did so.

He made twenty-nine illustrations for the text, all but two of which were reproduced in *St. Nicholas* (with shoes) and one of which (see p. 62) was only partly used. This Mark Twain Library edition incorporates all of them, drawing on the magazine as well as both the English and American editions to supply those omitted from *St. Nicholas.* The captions, although drawn from Mark Twain's text, were almost certainly provided by the illustrator. Mark Twain was unqualified in his praise of Beard's work, saying in 1894 that he was "the only man who can correctly illustrate my writings, for he not only illustrates the text, but he also illustrates my thoughts." On 16 October, having seen the first magazine installment, he wrote his daughter Clara: "I think Beard's pictures in 'Tom Sawyer Abroad,' in St Nicholas, are mighty good."

But the author remained dissatisfied with the magazine's text, and he therefore directed Hall *not* to rely on the *St. Nicholas* printing for the American book edition. Unfortunately, when he gave this order sometime in January 1894, Hall's typesetters had already prepared the first nine chapters from just that source. The American edition consequently reproduced the heavily bowdlerized *St. Nicholas* text for all but the last four chapters, which were based on the revised carbon-copy typescript that had not been edited by Mrs. Dodge. Hall also sent this revised carbon to Chatto & Windus, who used it for the first

English edition, incorporating most but not all of Mark Twain's revisions. None of the texts of *Tom Sawyer Abroad* published in Mark Twain's lifetime, therefore, accurately reproduced the text as he had finally revised it in 1892.

The text provided here is the only one ever to be based directly on the author's manuscript, which it follows faithfully except when he revised it on the typescript. Since none of the typescripts survives, Mr. Firkins has compared the manuscript with the three typesettings made from the typescripts in order to distinguish between editorial changes and the author's revisions. This text is the first to incorporate only those changes that Mark Twain himself made and to refrain from the impulse to "improve" his "spelling and punctuation." (For further details, see O M Brack, "Mark Twain in Knee Pants: The Expurgation of *Tom Sawyer Abroad*," *Proof* 2 [1972]: 145–151, and the introduction and notes to volume 4 in the Works of Mark Twain.)

TOM SAWYER, DETECTIVE

Mr. Firkins established the text of this story from five authoritative documents: (1) Mark Twain's manuscript for all but the last chapter, now in the Mark Twain Papers, The Bancroft Library, University of California at Berkeley; (2) a typescript of these chapters, revised by Mark Twain, MS P370A in the Department of Special Collections, Kenneth Spencer Research Library, University of Kansas; (3) the complete story as published in *Harper's New Monthly Magazine* in two installments, August and September 1896; (4) the complete story as published in *Tom Sawyer Abroad; Tom Sawyer, Detective and Other Stories* by Harper and Brothers in November 1896; and (5) the complete story as published in *Tom Sawyer, Detective, as Told by Huck Finn and Other Tales* by Chatto & Windus in December 1896. The following account is based on Mr. Firkins' introduction and notes, supplemented by documents in the Mark Twain Papers at Berkeley.

By the end of 1894 Mark Twain had drafted an early version of his story, now lost, which he called "Tom Sawyer's Mystery." He transformed this early version during the first three weeks of January 1895 into the present tale, lacking its concluding chapter. He ordered the manuscript typed, and then revised the typescript (now in the Kenneth Spencer Research Library at the University of Kansas). On 21 January 1895 he wrote the long final chapter in a single sitting and then had the whole story re-typed from his revised typescript and this new manuscript chapter. By 7 February, while still in Paris, he had extensively revised this second typescript and had had a third, clear or "fair copy" typescript (with carbon copy) made from it before sending both to New York. *Harper's Magazine* and Chatto & Windus were both provided with one of these fair copies to use for their texts. The Harpers set their book edition, however, from two other sources instead of the fair copy: chapters 1–7 from *Harper's Magazine*, and chapters 8–11 from the second, heavily revised typescript. Since only the earliest of these typescripts survives, Mr. Firkins has compared the three typesettings with the manuscript in order to distinguish typist's errors and editorial changes from the author's own revisions. He has also shown that Mark Twain made a few changes in proof for the English edition. For example, he deleted the footnote which he had earlier added to the second typescript: "Strange as the incidents of this story are, they are not inventions, but facts—even to the public confession of the accused. I take them from an old-time Swedish criminal trial, change the actors, and transfer the scene to America. I have added some details, but only a couple of them are important ones." On 26 October 1896 Mark Twain wrote to his English publisher, asking him to *"strike out the note which precedes 'Tom Sawyer Detective.'* . . . Doesn't it look like an attempt to make the reader believe true what I have failed to make *sound* true?" This and a few other changes were made in the English, but not in the American, edition.

The text provided here is the only one ever to be based directly on the author's manuscript, which it follows more faithfully than Mark Twain's typists and typesetters ever did. It is also the only text to incorporate all of Mark Twain's revisions, while excluding editorial changes imposed on him. And it is the first text since the *Harper's Magazine* version in 1896 to include the original illustrations by A. B. Frost. Mark Twain is not known to have commented on the illustrations for his story, but their subsequent omission in both English and American editions probably reflects the publishers' desire to cut costs, rather than any dissatisfaction of the author. Less than six months after "Tom Sawyer, Detective" appeared in *Harper's*, Mark Twain asked his American publisher to secure Frost's services for his next book, *Following the Equator*. "He is the best humorous artist that I know of, and . . . he told me 3 years ago that he had long had an ambition to make some illustrations for me."

I have altered the texts of the 1980 edition to correct transcription errors and, on four occasions, to take advantage of new evidence. The dedication Mark Twain wrote but failed to place in the American edition is supplied here because, as he wrote his wife, he had "instructed Mr. Hall to see to it that the second edition contains it." The manuscript reading "pow-wow" is restored because it now seems most likely that the typist misconstrued the word as "proud man" (3.14) and that this misreading was inadvertently accepted in all later texts. The manuscript reading "Mostem" (98.21) has, on the other hand, been corrected to "Moslem" (as in all printed texts) because it seems clear that Mark Twain inadvertently misspelled the word in his manuscript: Huck spells it correctly only ten words earlier in the same sentence and so cannot have misunderstood how to pronounce it. And the manuscript spelling "trapsing" in *Tom Sawyer, Detective* (108.10) has been restored, since omitting the first *i* ("traipsing") is not an error. The following correct readings from the two manuscripts are supplied: "time," for "time;" (55.14); "cuss." for "cuss!" (58.2); "Maine" for "Maine," (65.29); "ever" for "every" (79.11); "Sphynx" and "Sphynx's" for "Sphinx" and "Sphinx's" (89.38, 90.20, and 91.5); "fur" for "far" (107.15); "let" for "left" (108.39); "you;" for "you," (120.9); "hendering," for "hendering" (120.9); "looky-here" for "looky here" (134.3); "log cabin" for "log-cabin" (149.19); "sorry" for "sorry," (151.3); and "come" for "came" (153.6).

Robert H. Hirst
General Editor, Mark Twain Project
September 1981